W9-AUL-587

Though Ace was probably a factor, she reasoned, the strenuous walk was the cause of her rapid heartbeat—the exhilaration of simply being alive.

"Clarisse."

She turned around. Her breath caught. Her heartbeat increased. Ace had found a plot of grass and removed the contents of the bag he carried. Two boxed lunches sat on a plastic tablecloth, along with a bottle of sparkling water, a bowl of fruit and two plastic cups. She looked from the modest spread to the man who'd prepared it, catching the challenging yet vulnerable look in his eyes. She saw the jacked-up little boy he'd described the other night thrown into a world of wolves. And for the first time in a long time she imagined someone's feelings above her own.

She walked to stand in front of him, raised her lips for a quick kiss. "I've eaten in the finest restaurants in exotic places all over the world. But by far, this is sure to be my favorite meal."

She watched his eyes shift from conveying worry to relief. He pulled her into an embrace.

Dear Reader,

I landed the perfect first job at the age of sixteen as a cashier at a Sears Outlet store. Rarely did my first check make it home. Instead, I'd stash away cute clothes from the weekly shipments and cheerfully give my earnings right back to the store. My love of fashion inspired me to enroll at a junior college nearby for a degree in fashion merchandising and a career in clothing.

By my sophomore year, I was managing a small, chic boutique at the local mall. Great job, fun times, but my meager checks going back to the store instead of into the bank foretold a paltry future for this fashionista! So I switched careers and switched again and along the way fell into writing. But my love of the fashion world remains, so it was a joy to vicariously live there once again through London's story. And who knows? One day I might still own that chic boutique with one-of-a-kind fashions.

Zuri Day never stops dreaming…

Zuri

Lavish Loving

ZURI DAY

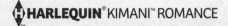

HARLEQUIN® KIMANI™ ROMANCE

If you purchased this book without a cover you should be aware
that this book is stolen property. It was reported as "unsold and
destroyed" to the publisher, and neither the author nor the
publisher has received any payment for this "stripped book."

Recycling programs
for this product may
not exist in your area.

ISBN-13: 978-0-373-86500-0

Lavish Loving

Copyright © 2017 by Zuri Day

All rights reserved. The reproduction, transmission or utilization of this
work in whole or in part in any form by any electronic, mechanical or
other means, now known or hereinafter invented, including xerography,
photocopying and recording, or in any information storage or retrieval
system, is forbidden without written permission. For permission please
contact Harlequin Kimani, 225 Duncan Mill Road, Toronto, Ontario
M3B 3K9, Canada.

This is a work of fiction. Names, characters, places and incidents are
either the product of the author's imagination or are used fictitiously,
and any resemblance to actual persons, living or dead, business establishments,
events or locales is entirely coincidental.

® and TM are trademarks of Harlequin Enterprises Limited or its corporate
affiliates. Trademarks indicated with ® are registered in the United States
Patent and Trademark Office, the Canadian Intellectual Property Office and in
other countries.

For questions and comments about the quality of this book please contact us
at CustomerService@Harlequin.com.

HARLEQUIN®
www.Harlequin.com

Printed in U.S.A.

Zuri Day is the national bestselling author of almost two dozen novels, including the popular Drakes of California series. Her books have earned her a coveted *Publishers Weekly* starred review and a Top Ten Pick out of all the romances featured in the spring 2014 edition. Day is a winner of the EMMA and African-American Literary Award Show Best Romance awards, among others, and a multiple *RT Book Reviews* Best Multicultural Fiction finalist. Book six in the Drakes of California series, *Crystal Caress,* was voted Book of the Year and garnered her yet another EMMA in 2016. Her work has been featured in several national publications including *RT Book Reviews*, *Publishers Weekly*, *Sheen*, *Juicy* and *USA TODAY*. She loves interacting with her fans, the DayDreamers, and when she sees them in person gives out free hugs! Contact her and find out more at zuriday.com.

Books by Zuri Day

Harlequin Kimani Romance

Diamond Dreams
Champagne Kisses
Platinum Promises
Solid Gold Seduction
Secret Silver Linings
Crystal Caress
Silken Embrace
Sapphire Attraction
Lavish Loving

Visit the Author Profile page
at Harlequin.com for more titles.

Anything worth having is worth fighting for.
When the fight is for love, it's worth so much more.
Facing fears, beating foes, minor problems, you see.
When all ends with a chance to love lavishly.

Chapter 1

Was that…? No. Couldn't be. Not here in Temecula, California, a place London Drake only knew about because that's where her cousins lived. Nothing against the town. It was quaint, cozy and home to dozens of Southern California's celebrated vineyards as well as Drake Wines Resort and Spa, where she was now. But there was no way former celebrity model, current fashion mogul and any woman's favorite fantasy, Ace Montgomery, could be here. Was there?

These rapid-fire thoughts collided with one another as London quickly shifted her body for a second glimpse. That she was on an escalator was totally forgotten. She grabbed the rail to keep her balance. The unconscious step backward as she attempted to get a better view almost created a domino effect that would have felled the women behind her. The group reached their destination unscathed, but the stumble hadn't gone unnoticed.

"Are you okay?"

"I'm fine, Diamond. Just thought I saw someone I knew, that's all."

Diamond Drake Wright, London's first cousin and a company executive, took the lead as the ladies entered Wine, the trendy new bar on the second floor of the resort's boutique hotel. She greeted the hostess, waved away the offer to be escorted to their reserved booth and led the ladies to a roped-off area that featured artfully arranged seating—velvet love seats, matching chairs, fabric-tufted benches and an array of unique-looking tables to hold food and drink. The area was positioned on the small side of the L-shaped room, tucked behind the hostess station, and offered a modicum of privacy in this popular public place.

London sat on a champagne-colored love seat. Her sister-in-law Quinn plopped down beside her. "Sure you need a drink? Your clumsiness gives the impression that you've knocked back a couple behind our backs already."

London gave Quinn the kind of look that required no words but conveyed *shut the hell up* quite nicely.

"She saw a cute guy," Diamond offered as she too sat on the love seat.

"Oh." Quinn drew out the word meaningfully. "That makes sense. It wouldn't be the first time London has fallen head over heels for a man."

"Oh, be quiet." London swatted Quinn's arm as the women around her laughed. "I saw someone I thought I knew. Not just some cute guy." The ladies shared dubious looks between them. "Did y'all forget the industry I work in?" London huffed. "And that I've modeled with some of the best-looking men on the planet? If I fell over every time I saw one, I'd live on the floor."

True statement. London's supermodel-turned-celebrity

lifestyle had allowed her to not only work with but to date the types of men most women only saw on glossy magazine pages, a computer screen or TV. Like her ex Maxwell Tata, the handsome, successful A-list director. Like the man who'd almost made her fall head over heels tonight...for a second time.

But he wasn't there. Couldn't be. He was busy running a fashion empire in San Francisco. It had been years since they'd talked, but that's what she'd heard. And that he'd gotten engaged. She hadn't heard or read about a wedding, though. Was that why he was here? To marry his fiancée? Wouldn't that be the irony of ironies, if he was here for a wedding and she for a funeral?

A couple more minutes, another sip of wine and London had successfully convinced herself that she hadn't seen Ace, but seeing a man who could be his twin took her back to the magical night they'd met. And made love. And spent the next two days in a fantasy world before reality took them in different directions.

It was her eighteenth-birthday weekend, and London, who'd been discovered by a modeling scout the year before, couldn't have imagined a more perfect celebration. She'd just finished her first hectic, whirlwind week in the city that had inspired her name. Her family had flown to England to watch her walk the runway. After enjoying a private dinner prepared by a world-renowned chef, she'd said goodbye to the Drakes and been whisked away to an exclusive party held just for her. Incomparable, the number one modeling agency in the world, had pulled out all the stops to make the night memorable. They'd rented a castle for the grand affair, a testament to the fact she was the agency's queen bee. The guest list read like a who's who of fashion, entertainment and sports. One of the guests was Ace Montgomery, a runway veteran at the ripe old age of twenty-one, whose sexy underwear ads had made him one of the most recognizable, bankable and sought-after models on the globe. London had not been immune to his charm, had salivated over his pictures like any red-blooded woman would. His eyes had seared her from across the room, caused a shiver down her spine and a flutter in other places. Throughout the evening she caught him looking. Or vice versa. But he didn't approach. She guessed him to be arrogant and aloof, so when chance brought them together in the long hallway of one of the castle's quieter wings, his shy, somewhat corny nature had thrown her off guard.

"Hi." His voice was softer than she'd imagined it would be, and raspy.

"Hey, what's up?"

He stopped. She didn't.

"London, right?"

Already steps away from him, she paused, turned and answered while walking back to where he stood. "Yeah."

"Last name Bridges?"

She gave him an eye roll.

"Fog?"

A hint of a smile, just barely.

"London lightbulb? On account of how bright you're shining?" The comment combined with the doofus-looking expression on his face made London laugh out loud.

"You're stupid!"

"Sometimes." He held out his hand. "Ace Montgomery."

Her eyes slid from his eyes to the extended hand and back. They were the only things that moved. "Like I don't know who you are."

"No, like I'm just being courteous and greeting you formally." His arm remained outstretched.

She placed her small hand in his extralarge one. An electrical shock ran through them.

"Whoa!" Ace snatched back his hand. "Did you feel that?"

"That's what happens when you touch a lightbulb," London deadpanned. "Nice talking to you."

London walked away without looking back. He was exquisite to look at, but the shine faded when he opened his mouth.

That was her first impression. Later that night her publicist yielded her seat in the crowded room so that London and Ace could sit and "get to know each other." No coincidence, London knew. Her publicist was strategizing. Always on the hunt for a story that would keep her client in the public eye. The flashbulbs that went off shortly afterward confirmed this belief. The conversation that followed led to a better second impression.

In the next half hour Ace came out of his shy, quiet shell and became quite engaging. He flawlessly handled the stream of admirers that came his way but continued to make London his central focus. Impressive. Not easy to do.

Photo ops and interviews pulled them away from each other. When London saw him an hour and two glasses of wine later, she asked the question that had tickled the tip of her tongue all night.

"I have a question for you?"

"Sure."

"Is the bulge beneath those sexy black boxers you made famous real or concocted?"

"*Concocted*—good word."

"You know, like from a sock or a certain vegetable or something."

A bit of the cockiness London expected oozed through

Ace's megawatt smile. "No, baby. What you see in those pictures is grade-Ace beef."

London's look was dubious.

"Don't believe me?"

"Nope."

"Want to see for yourself?"

A slight lick of his lips brought moisture to a set of hers.

"Sure, why not?"

He took her hand, led her to an empty bedroom and locked the door. They didn't come out for two days.

"London…" Quinn softly nudged her.

"Hmm?"

"Stop thinking about the cute guy and pick up your glass. Diamond wants to propose a toast."

"Oh. Okay." London lifted her champagne flute, unaware of when it was placed there or filled.

Quinn and Diamond shared a glance, but she said nothing more.

While others shared a glass from a bottle of the vineyard's premiere champagne, Diamond, its namesake, lifted a glass of sparkling white grape juice. "To our dearest Papa Dee. May he have half as good a life in heaven as he had here on earth."

"All of those young beautiful angels in heaven? Papa won't be resting at all!"

"Right!" London chuckled at Katrina's comment. They'd crossed paths at their large biannual family reunions but this was her first time really hanging out with this funny, feisty and fearless cousin from North Carolina. For equally carefree London, it was love at first hug.

Katrina's statement brought much-needed levity to what had been a sad and exhausting day. More than five hundred people, including over one hundred members of the Drake clan, had gathered at the resort to pay last respects to the family patriarch, David "Papa Dee" Drake, who at the blessed age of 104 had earned his angel wings. Three of London's cousins and two of her in-laws had decided to separate from the throng of friends and relatives still at the resort for some quieter, more intimate bonding before tomorrow, when everyone would start going their separate ways. For a while, funny stories of Papa Dee and recollections from the past two days dominated conversation. But eventually it came back around to London and the cute guy, courtesy of Katrina.

"So, London, who'd you see earlier that had you falling on the stairs?"

"Hopefully not another stalker," Quinn offered.

"No stalker, thank God."

And never again, she hoped. London still got chills when she thought of the man who'd followed her from Paris to Milan, all the way to a hotel room in New York. He'd been arrested, deported and jailed, so it couldn't be him. And again, London thought, thank God.

Burying the thought, she turned to her cousin. "And I didn't fall, Katrina, not even close. Not even when I climbed the tourist-unfriendly mountain to Papa Dee's final resting place in my five-inch Choos."

"Which is why I strongly suggested you choose a different, more appropriate shoe." The mere implication of a resort imperfection caused marketing and PR director Diamond Drake Wright to bristle, though the discomfort of being eight months pregnant might have contributed, too. "And while only you could have turned that earlier stumble into a graceful, even sexy, curtsy type of thing, you're avoiding Katrina's question. So spill the tea. Who was it, and don't say just some guy, because we're not buying that at all."

London shrugged. "Wish I had something juicy to bring to this obviously bored table, but whoever the person was reminded me of a casual friend who lived in Europe. No one you guys would know."

"Oh, good," Diamond said, looking around to ensure her next words would be as discreet as she intended. "Because Ace Montgomery is here but wants his stay to remain private."

"Ace Mon—" Katrina began to exclaim.

"Shh!" Diamond interrupted.

"The model?" Diamond's sister-in-law Marissa was the quiet one in this group, but even her whisper held excitement.

"The one in the sexy underwear ads!" Katrina whispered. "Oh, my goodness, what's his room number? It's about to go down!"

Katrina began to rise.

"No, you're about to sit down." Diamond caught Katrina's arm and gave her the don't-mess-with-the-pregnant-lady eye. Katrina dutifully sat down. "That's confidential information only shared with family." She looked at Katrina. "Something that on second thought may not have been the best idea. This baby obviously has my brain as cramped as my organs feel right now."

She leaned back to relieve the pressure from her expanded girth. Finding none, she stood.

So did London. "Are you okay?"

"Just too uncomfortable to keep sitting." She rubbed her stomach. "I think little Jackson is ready for bed."

London reached for Diamond's purse. "I'll walk you to your car."

"That's okay, cousin. Stay here and enjoy yourself."

"I was headed to the bathroom anyway."

"There's one right behind you."

"I'd rather use the one in the lobby." Diamond grunted. "Stop being so independent. I'm going to walk you down."

Two steps out of Wine and the conversation continued. "No."

"What?" London asked Diamond, her face a study in innocence.

"What?" Diamond parroted. "I'm not stupid. Earlier, it was Ace you saw, and by your reaction whatever happened in Europe with this *friend*—" she made air quotes with her fingers "—wasn't as casual as you claimed. Now try and deny it."

"Dang, was I that transparent?"

"No, I'm that good at reading people. Especially those on the prowl in hotels."

"I am hardly on the prowl."

"Oh, really?"

"Yes, really. I don't look for men. They look for me."

"Then you wouldn't be interested in any information I'd have about him. His room number, for instance? Or that he checked in alone?"

They reached the hotel entrance and stepped outside.

"Okay, what is it?"

"No, you're probably right. No need to share information you won't even use."

"I might use it. Make a phone call. Have a chat."

"Just a phone call, huh? You can do that through the front desk. Just dial zero and ask for him."

"I don't want the hotel staff in my business."

Diamond raised a brow. "Or your relatives?"

"What's the room number?" London huffed.

"Oh, darn. Look at our observant and efficient valet staff. Already here with my car." Diamond spoke to the young man who held the car door open and got inside.

"Diamond!"

Diamond laughed, blew a kiss. "Sweet dreams, London. See you tomorrow at brunch!"

London hid her exasperation behind a smile and waved goodbye. Her frustration was gone before Diamond's car left the hotel driveway. It had been a few months since she'd broken things off with Maxwell and London was more than ready for some horizontal aerobics. Nothing serious, though. A friend with several inches' worth of benefits. Or someone like the hotel guest who reminded her of the bad-boy blond Max had recently made famous. Yesterday, he'd seen through her thin wig-and-shades disguise and requested a selfie. Someone like him would be fun. Not someone for whom she'd once had feelings and who was engaged—even married, as far as she knew.

Even though he checked in alone?

Yes, even though.

No Ace. Keep it moving. Got it.

She crossed the lobby to the ladies' room. The marble-and-brass appointments made even a simple trip to the loo a luxury. London entered one of six stalls and handled her business. She was just about to exit when she heard more women enter, whispering and giggling. London didn't want to take a chance on being recognized, and at a towering six feet plus in her ever-present five-inch heels, she was hard to miss. That and the fact that over the past five years her oval face, big brown eyes and naturally plump lips had graced the cover of every major magazine in the world. Throughout the Papa Dee celebrations, most had respected her privacy and the situation and left her alone. Not sure that would happen now. She didn't feel like socializing with strangers but didn't want to be rude. So she muted her phone and silently scrolled through a social media site, waiting for them to be gone.

"Oh, my gosh! He's even better looking in person!"

London's ears perked up. Her head raised, too.

"I know, right? I got a selfie!"

A rustling sound followed as London assumed the speaker was digging through her bag.

"Mr. Hotness in the hot flesh."

She must have found it.

"Darn it! I'm jealous! You should have asked for one in his undies."

"I know, right!"

A high five sounded. London scowled.

"Ooh, I'd do anything to be Ellen right now. Fine man like that on vacation all alone."

"Alone? I thought I read that he was married."

"Engaged, but they broke up."

London's brow raised. *Oh, really now.* Bathroom breaking news had just gotten more interesting.

"He scheduled a massage?"

"Yes. She gets to massage that fine mass of muscle for a whole hour!"

"Shut up! Why was she the lucky choice?"

"She's one of the best in the business. It probably doesn't hurt that she's married, a grandmother and twice his age. The hotel wouldn't want any scandal."

London heard a sigh.

"Guess I'll have to content myself with changing his sheets and inhaling the cologne lingering on them."

"Is he in the Champagne bungalow?"

"No, the Pinot Noir. His massage is at noon. I'd love to be a fly on the wall."

All that talk about Ace's sexiness made London replace thoughts about boundaries with memories of Ace's hard body. In that moment she determined that tomorrow at noon, she was going to be that fly.

Chapter 2

They'd all been right. Especially Tyler, one of two business partners with whom Ace had opened Out of the Box, a fashion design company. They'd debuted with a menswear line known to the world as OTB Him. The launch had been as exhausting as it was successful. Ace had worked too hard for too long. He needed a break.

"You know it's bad when you stop getting on my nerves and start getting on your own," Tyler Dent had quipped last Tuesday after Ace fired a talented designer and scrapped a clothing direction months in the making. "You're frickin' overstressed, man. Either take a vacation or find another partner."

Ace had responded with a few choice words, an upward flip of a certain finger and a door slam to punctuate his exit. He'd apologized later that evening and Dent, as Ace called him, in characteristic fashion, shook it off, bought him a beer and reiterated his ultimatum. The next day Ace had tasked his assistant with finding him a quiet, private place to unwind, something outside Northern California but no farther than a two-hour drive or hour-long airplane ride away. Among the several links she sent was the place he was now, Drake Wines Resort and Spa. The award-winning hotel and winery had appealed to him for several reasons. The private, freestanding bungalows they featured was only one of them.

Back from an invigorating two-mile run, Ace entered the expansive two-bedroom abode and headed straight for the master suite. He'd been forbidden from calling the office, and to abide by these wishes had left his phone in the room. He grabbed it, tapped the icon for his company email and strolled into the kitchen while the newest messages synced in. After opening a bottle of water and taking a long swig, he sat at the table to read through the day's mail.

The name he'd hoped to see popped out at him. He opened the message, read the quick note and tapped the clip to open attachments. After a couple flicks of his thumbs, he breathed a deep sigh of relief. He hadn't regretted firing the talented but temperamental designer this week. He had been doubtful about finding another one who could bring the new line Ace envisioned to life. But Lucien, the teenager who'd won a TV show design contest, was just that guy. His portfolio was everything Ace had hoped for and then some—as fresh, innovative and daring as the styles that had won him first prize. The new OTB fashion line, this one for women, would definitely turn heads. All they needed now was the right muse to wear it.

He replied to the email, forwarded the images to the partners and then, satisfied that his company actually could go twenty-four hours without his direct involvement, slipped out of his running shoes, shorts and tee and stepped into the shower. He leaned against the cool marble, a stark yet welcome contrast to the warm water streaming over his body. He stepped under the rain showerhead and let the water flow through his close-cropped curls, trickle over his brow, angular nose, full lips and dimpled chin, across his broad shoulders, down his rock-hard chest and back, pooling at his size fourteens before swirling into and down the drain. He increased the heat even more and turned on the multijet system. Soon, water shot to his body from eight different jets. A full-body massage was scheduled in just ten minutes, but this torrential pounding was going to be hard to beat.

Five minutes later he reluctantly stepped out of the shower, dried off six feet of chocolate perfection and donned a downy, soft cashmere robe with matching slippers. He was hungry and wished he scheduled enough time for a meal before his massage, but the ringing sound of a brass knocker proved the thought had come too late. He walked to the door and opened it.

A stout, pleasant-looking woman stood in the doorway. Ace was relieved. He was at the resort to relax, not fight off overzealous fans. From the looks of the woman who stood before him, he was safe.

"Mr. Montgomery?"

"Yes."

"Hi, I'm Ellen, here for your massage appointment."

"Please, come in."

Ellen entered, pulling an oversize canvas bag on wheels. The strap of another bag made of the same material rested on her shoulder. She placed the larger bag on the floor and the smaller one on top of it.

"That's the massage table?" Ellen nodded. "The whole table is in that small bag?"

This elicited a smile and another nod. "I assure you that it's comfortable and durable, yet light and easily transportable. Top of the line."

"If you say so. Would you like a drink, a glass of water, perhaps?"

"No, nothing. Thank you."

"I hear you're one of the best."

"I try. You signed up for the Swedish/deep tissue combo. Is that still your choice?"

Ace nodded. "I think that'll work."

"Very well. I will get set up in the master suite."

In short order the therapist returned and stated that she was ready to begin. "Please remove your robe, climb between the sheets and let me know when it's fine for me to enter the room."

"Will do."

Ace found humor in Ellen's serious nature and entered his suite with a smile. The shades had been pulled, he noted, with aromatic candles placed strategically around the room. An array of oils were positioned on a nearby table. New age music wafted from an iPod. Five minutes and Ellen had turned the master suite into a spa room.

He removed the robe, tossed it on the bed and climbed aboard a table, which, surprisingly, was as light, sturdy and comfortable as Ellen had claimed. As he settled himself between the sheets, a sound resembling a knock reached his ears. He paused and heard a muted conversation. *Probably the housekeeper.* Ace settled himself beneath the sheet, placed his head into the headrest and anticipated with pleasure a much-needed massage.

A moment later, there was a knock on his door. "Come in."

"Ready?"

"Yes, Ellen. I'm ready. Come on in."

"Just relax. Close your eyes."

Ace's brow furled. The voice sounded deeper, forced, her accent more pronounced. He dismissed the suspicion as quickly as it came. In his twenty-nine years he'd learned to question everything. But he was on vacation at a reputable, first-class resort and spa in a town he'd not heard of until clicking the link. If there was any place he could relax and feel safe it was here, in Temecula, California, in a bungalow named after a wine.

Two seconds after Ellen moved toward him, the frown returned. There was a smell—citrusy, spicy—that had not been there moments before. While most men wouldn't have noticed, Ace had always been a lover of fragrance, especially when inhaled from the skin of a fine woman. Had Ellen whipped out the perfume before reentering his boudoir? Was there a little freak behind the formal facade? He almost laughed out loud. Still, his senses, especially those of smell and sound, were heightened in the darkened room. The music shifted from a haunting, piano-driven melody to a sensuous-sounding serenade led by a sultry sax. He heard hands being rubbed briskly together to warm up the oil. Felt the slightest of hesitations before two soft palms pressed against his upper back. Small hands. Smaller than he'd imagined Ellen's would be. Softer, too. The oil was warm and soothing. Expert fingers began to knead the healing oil into his skin, across his back and shoulders. He closed his eyes, told himself he'd earned the right to relax.

Her fingers were slender but surprisingly strong. She massaged and nudged and kneaded his tight muscles into submission and glided her palms softly, slowly, almost lovingly, across his body. A swirl of air kissed his skin as the sheet was pulled lower, exposing the dimples just above his hard butt. Palms came together briskly. Ace could feel the heat of them hovering just above his buns.

Come on, Ellen. Don't get shy now!

She didn't. Not at all. Instead she pulled the sheet down farther, exposed his cheeks and slapped his bare ass.

"What the—" A shocked Ace turned and sat up in a single motion. "London?"

London was smiling, but his expression made her laugh out loud.

"Where's Ellen? How..." The sheet slid to the floor. Ace cupped his hands over, well, as much of himself as he could.

London tried to stop laughing. "Don't worry about that, big boy. Nothing I haven't seen before. Besides, there's no modesty in modeling. You know that."

He rolled off the table, reached for the sheet and hurriedly wrapped it around him, totally flustered. "What are you doing here?"

"Until a second or two ago, I thought I was giving you a darn good massage."

"This isn't funny, London. How'd you get in my room?"

London was as calm as Ace was rattled. She sat on the four-poster king-size bed and leaned back on her elbows. "You're not happy to see me?"

Though she appeared to him as a vision of pure loveliness, he looked at her like she'd grown a horn in the middle of her forehead. "It's not about being happy or not. My being here is supposed to be confidential. How'd you know I was here?"

"I have my ways. It's not like I'm a stranger, Ace. I'm a friend, who you're treating quite rudely at the moment."

"Forgive my lack of manners, London, but I thought

a hotel employee just smacked my ass and then found out, no, the therapist has been knocked off by a friend of mine who broke into my room!"

"Well, it wasn't a hotel employee. It was me. So calm down. Where's the guy I met seven years ago who talked like a dork and then showed me his penis?"

"He grew up."

"Good for you." She could walk out the door right now, but that would feel too much like running away. So she shifted the energy and her expression with a smile. "It's been forever since I've seen you. We've got a lot of catching up to do." She glanced suggestively at the bed. "Don't I get a hug?"

Ace looked at the bed and back at London, who wore a formfitting maxi. He took a step, tripped on the sheet and almost bared his goods again. "In there," he said, pointing toward the living room.

The lack of cordiality put London back in a huff. "Never mind. It's clear I'm not welcome, so I'll leave you alone." She strode out of the room.

Ace was right behind her. "London, wait."

She stopped but didn't turn around.

"You shocked the heck out of me, okay? Give me a minute to put some clothes on."

A slow, deliberate turn and then dark, daring eyes stared at him. "Are you sure about that?" Ace sighed. "Forget it. Jeez, I was just kidding. You act as though you're not happy to see me."

"I'm very glad to see you, London. I just need to put on some clothes."

He gave her a hug and a kiss to her forehead, then he pulled away before a certain part of his anatomy betrayed him and revealed just how much.

Chapter 3

London strolled over to the large picture window that let in a picturesque view of the Temescal Mountains. The commanding peaks reminded her of Switzerland and a cottage near her boarding school she and her friends would sneak out to when they wanted to meet up with boys. Her senior year, just after turning seventeen, she went on a trip to Paris and got discovered by Incomparable, one of the top modeling agencies in the world. A year later she met Ace and had her world rocked off its axis.

Her phone vibrated in the bag that rested against her thigh. It was a text from Diamond.

It's brunch. You're late.

London glanced toward the bedroom and typed a quick reply.

Busy. Can't come. Talk later. BTW... I'm always late.

Her thumb hadn't left the send button before she heard the padding of bare feet across the dark hardwood floor. Slipping the phone into her bag, she turned around and was met by the confident, carefree Ace that she remembered. But if he hoped to make himself less desirable by covering up with a pair of low-riding jeans and a black OTB tee, he failed. Miserably. The way London looked him up and down expressed that louder than words ever could.

"Come here, you." He opened his arms.

London crossed the room in a walk worthy of the runway and stepped into his embrace. "I'm glad you left the jerk in the bedroom and brought out the Ace that I know."

Her teasing smile rendered the barb harmless.

His hug was heartfelt and even though she'd spent several pleasurable minutes rubbing oil over his body, she relished the chance to touch him again. "It's good to see you," she said, dropping her hands to squeeze his butt, one of her favorite parts of his anatomy.

He caught her wrists and pulled her hands away. "Still the troublemaker, I see."

"I try."

"What are you doing here?" they asked each other.

"Oh, no. That's my question." Ace reached for her hand and led them to the couch. He sat and pulled her down with him. "Now out with it. The truth. What's this about?"

London leaned against the comfy couch, enjoying Ace's suspicious discomfort a bit more than she should. When his eyes turned stormy, she knew she'd toyed with him long enough.

"It's pure coincidence," she said with a shrug. "I came here for a funeral."

"A funeral. At a luxury hotel."

"I guess without explanation that does sound pretty

weird. It was for my great-grandfather. He owned this land, planted the first vineyards and nurtured the idea of the full-scale winery that you see today."

"This resort belongs to your family?"

London nodded. "My first cousins."

Ace's head fell against the cushions. "This is crazy! I pick this place expecting to see no one I know, and it's owned by a friend. What are the chances?"

"I was shocked to see you, too."

Ace raised his head. "When'd you see me?"

London told him about last night's events. "I started to call but wasn't sure of the reception I'd get. But I really wanted to see you. Alone. So when I heard about the massage appointment, there it was, my way in."

"Ellen never should have agreed to let you in my room. You could be a serial killer! I'm going to report her."

"Please don't. I offered her a believable story and a ridiculous amount of money to take her place. When it comes to something I want, I can be pretty persuasive. So, please, can we keep this between us? I'd hate for her to lose her job, and knowing my cousins, that's exactly what would happen."

"How much was this visit worth to you?"

"A lot."

"How much?"

"That's between me and Ellen. Telling you would go straight to your head."

"That much, huh?"

"My lips are sealed."

Ace turned toward London, crossed his arms and nestled into the couch's corner.

"So even though years ago you told me you had none, your last name is Drake."

"You obviously didn't do your research. One click on an internet search engine could have told you that."

"Like it could have told me whether or not your real name is London? Not that I'm into the whole search engine stalking thing."

The teasing returned. "Absolutely, and I wouldn't mind a stalker as fine as you. I'm willing to tell you, but only if there's something for me in return."

Ace's eyes turned dark, this time with desire instead of ire. "I'm sure I can think of something."

Was it London's imagination, or did the room's temperature just rise?

"My full name is Clarisse Alana Drake. I legally added London when I turned eighteen."

Ace's gaze remained intense as he gazed at her. "Clarisse."

The name floated off his tongue like a song, caressed her ears like raw silk.

"That's a beautiful name. Why'd you change it?"

London shrugged. "Boredom. Errant impulse. Teenage rebellion. Take your pick."

"Clarisse is a beautiful name, though I can understand why you'd use another."

London's brow creased. "Why?"

"It doesn't fit you. That name is for a woman who is demure, sweet, refined, quiet."

London crossed her arms.

"And that's not me?" Asked demurely, of course.

"No, it's not. You're a hellion who bribed a hotel employee to take advantage of a naked man. A woman named Clarisse would never do that."

"But a woman named London would?"

"A woman named London would, and did."

"I guess I did, huh? But I haven't gotten the chance to take advantage of your nakedness…yet."

Ace shook his head. "You're incorrigible."

"So it's my turn for answers. What are you doing here? Last I heard you were running a design house in San Francisco. And engaged."

"You heard correctly. A couple partners and I opened OTB three years ago. The engagement didn't work out."

"I can relate."

"Yeah, I saw somewhere that you and the director called it quits."

"I thought you weren't the search engine stalker type?"

"I didn't search out the information. If I remember correctly it was a major network's breaking news."

London nodded. No denying the truth. "I get that OTB stands for outside the box, and your looks certainly are that. But why didn't you name it Ace something or other?"

"There are already several Ace lines. Plus, this is a collaborative effort. It's not all about me."

"Is that why you left modeling, and Europe, so suddenly?"

"I didn't leave suddenly, even though it seemed that way. I'd planned my exit, had charted the next course of my life." His gaze slid to her then away. "It obviously didn't matter to you, anyway."

London sat up in genuine surprise. "Why would you say that?"

"Don't put on that act like you would have cared. You used me up in a one-night stand and walked away without a backward glance."

"Um, I seem to remember the situation quite differently, and it wasn't a one-night stand…it was two."

"How do you remember it?"

"You said you'd call me. You never did."

Ace rubbed a hand across the shadow of his unshaven jaw. "I don't remember that. It was a long time ago, though, so you might be right. But so what. You could have called me."

"Negative, darling. That's the desperate move of a thirsty girl."

"Not necessarily. It could be the move of a strong, independent woman who knows what she wants. Like the one who bogarted her way into my bedroom."

London gave a noncommittal brow raise, nothing more.

"Besides, that wasn't the last time you saw me. If you had feelings about the weekend we shared, why didn't you say something?"

"Why didn't you?"

Ace sighed. "Young. Foolish. I was really digging you, London. But life moved fast back then—a little too fast. By the time I met you, I'd already been on that whirlwind grind for six years. The underwear campaign had blown up into something none of us expected. What was supposed to be a six-month magazine and billboard ad turned into commercials, public appearances, people grabbing at me from every direction."

"Well…if you were digging me so much, you should have let me know. That's what a strong man does…goes after what he wants."

"I'll keep that in mind." Another look at her, his gaze intense. "Is that what the director did?"

"Max and I met at a party. I've been working on making the transition from modeling to acting for a while. Asked him for pointers. He suggested I star in his next movie." She shrugged. "Things went from there."

"So what happened that made y'all break up? You couldn't act or what?"

"Whatever, fool!" London reached for a decorative pillow and swung. He grabbed it, laughing.

"Max has a Jekyll and Hyde quality. He can be as charming and debonair as he can be manipulative and controlling. It was an exciting lifestyle but not one I could see myself in for the rest of my life. So I ended the relationship."

"Got marriage on the mind, huh? That surprises me."

"I'm full of surprises." She wriggled her brows, then got serious. "But being ready to get married isn't one of them."

Now that the shock of seeing her had worn off, the conversation between them flowed as easily as London remembered from past encounters. She relaxed against the opposite couch arm and idly twirled a curl.

"Yeah, everybody wanted Ace Montgomery. I remember that. How old were you back then, at the height of the underwear frenzy?"

"Twenty-one."

"Really? I thought you were older."

"How old are you?"

"Now? Twenty-five, with a birthday coming up."

"When?"

"August."

Ace nodded. "Planning on being on time for this celebration? You were known for being a tardy model back in the day."

"How'd you know that?"

"The industry talks."

"Have you ever booked fifteen shows during fashion week? Been pulled in every direction at the same time?" She didn't give him a chance to respond. "Besides, I work hard to be the best walker on the runway. I'm worth the wait."

"Had I been the designer and you weren't on time, there would have been consequences."

"Sounds like something I might have enjoyed." Ace fixed her with a scowl. She laughed while making the mental observation that a screwed-up face shouldn't look so sexy.

"So, you're what…twenty-nine, thirty?"

"Twenty-nine."

A loud, unmistakable sound filled the silence.

"Dang, is that your stomach?"

Ace's sheepish look made London laugh. "Sorry about that. I'm starving. Went for a run and didn't schedule enough time between appointments to eat."

"I haven't eaten, either. Let's go get something."

"Naw, I don't feel like getting out. The food here is amazing. The chef is a foodie genius from the Caribbean. I think I'll place an order for them to bring here."

"In that case," London said as she slithered over to his side of the couch, "why don't we start with dessert first?"

She was halfway on him, leaning in for a kiss when strong hands gripping her shoulders stopped her progress. "Stop acting like London. I want to get to know Clarisse."

London sat back in a huff, attitude evident.

Ace was unmoved. His posture remained casual and relaxed, but his next words were firm. "That strong man you mentioned earlier? You're looking at one. And we not only go after what we want, we plan when the party will happen. And then we lead the dance."

Chapter 4

There are circumstances in life that sometimes derail even a strong man's plans. That happened when London was summoned first by her cousin and then by her mother to return to the Drake mansion and bid some of the relatives who were leaving goodbye. Their impromptu lunch date was changed to a late dinner date instead and Ace was able to keep the original appointment on his itinerary—the one that he'd been ready to cancel in a heartbeat for a certain spoiled, entitled, irresistible woman named London—no, Clarisse.

His celebrity hidden behind a Raiders baseball cap and shades, Ace climbed into a golf cart for a tour of the winery. It would be conducted by the company's vintner, Dexter Drake. This was a rare occurrence. Normally the wine shop manager performed this task. But as life would have it, Dexter was a fan of the OTB line, with several of their designer duds lining his closet. So when he heard Ace was taking the tour, he offered to conduct it.

"It's really great to meet you, man," Dexter said once they took off. "Your designs are amazing. They fit my personality and style to a T."

"Thank you, Dexter. I appreciate that."

"Are you the designer?"

"I'm the visionary behind what people are wearing, but can't claim total ownership of the final pieces. I sketch out what's in my head and hand it over to a team of amazing designers who then add their own spin that often takes the look to a whole other level. In the end it's a collaborative effort."

"Whatever you're doing is working. I never thought I'd go for the double-breasted look again, but the new spin with the super narrow lapel, short coat and high-waisted slacks… Genius."

"Thanks, brother."

Dexter's phone rang. "Excuse me a moment."

For Ace the call was a welcome interruption. Dexter seemed like a nice guy and all, but Ace's mind was consumed with London. She'd acted miffed that he hadn't called her. Had she actually been hurt, or was that just an act? The way he remembered it, she couldn't have cared less. He recalled how he'd felt the first time he saw her—stunned by her beauty, aroused by her fire, frightened by the intense feelings her presence evoked. She'd walked in the room as if she owned it and brightened the whole place. She was carefree, obnoxious, bubbly and bold. Quiet by nature, suspicious by life, he'd immediately wanted to know her. But her largesse had reduced him to the gangly, acne-prone preteen he was before a six-inch growth spurt and a face-cleansing regimen had begun his transformation. He wanted to approach her, but to say he'd been intimidated would not have been a stretch. They'd flirted from opposite sides of the room.

She'd seemed interested. He still didn't approach. One of the setbacks to being a teenage heartthrob—no time to perfect the rap game. All the women he'd been involved with had come to him.

So their chance meeting in the hallway had been perfect. Even though he'd begun the conversation with a lame comment about her name. Thankfully, she hadn't cared. Much. Later, when her publicist brought them together, he'd been more relaxed. They'd clicked. Most of the night he'd asked the questions. Then...she'd asked one. It led to their finding an empty room in the huge castle her agency had rented out and exploring every inch of each other's bodies for forty-eight hours, interrupted only once to eat and recharge their batteries. But then he'd gone back to the United States on tour and she'd become the toast of Incomparable, and they'd lost touch. A few more casual meetings had followed, but never a chance to reconnect more intimately.

Then he'd met his ex-fiancée, the one who'd stolen his heart and tried to steal his money. That betrayal sent him home to Oakland, California, to lick his wounds. There, a conversation with his stepfather led to Ace giving his career path and his life serious thought. He'd renegotiated his modeling contracts, gone back to school and met Tyler. He gave Tyler a portfolio of designs, Tyler found Mira, Mira found money. The three created Out of the Box, trademarked the terms *Himwear* and *Herwear*, and introduced the first line of OTB Him three years ago. At next month's fashion week in New York City they'd unveil a new line—OTB Her. So here he chilled in a town called Temecula, pondering the perfect woman who could give life to this daring new line. And supermodel London walked into his bedroom. For Ace this was more than a coincidence. This was a sign. A dangerous, tempting, high-maintenance sign. A signal sure to rock the steady, predictable world he'd created since calling off the wedding with his ex and regaining control of his finances. Was he ready to bring such an unpredictable element into his life? Ace didn't know, but he was damned sure going to find out.

London stepped into Katrina's outstretched arms. "It was a pleasure reconnecting with you, too!" They rocked back and forth in a giant bear hug. She stepped back but kept her arms around her new favorite cousin. "Promise me you'll keep in touch."

"Oh, trust and believe I'm going to do that. You've got connections to some fine-ass men and one of them needs to be my husband!"

"Ha! I don't know about all that, but if you come up north, I promise to show you a good time."

"I'll hold you to that promise."

The women hugged again. London smiled and waved as Katrina, her brother, sister-in-law, niece, nephew and parents got into the limo that would take them to San Diego and one of two airports closest to the resort. Over the next hour, she shared farewells with other family members also leaving, some to San Diego and others to Ontario, the other major airport nearby. There were lots of hugs, a few tears and plenty of vows to stay in touch. In death, much as he had in life, Papa Dee had placed emphasis on the value of family and strengthened the tribal bond.

Shortly after the last limo pulled away, London jumped into one of several golf carts parked in the lot and headed over to Diamond's house. Built on the land by her construction company owner husband, Jackson Wright, it was a commanding design that seamlessly blended contemporary modern with Spanish and Mediterranean influences, filled with designer, exotic and top-of-the-line pieces. Along the way she passed several guesthouses, where some of the extended family had stayed, the home of Diamond's older brother Donovan and his wife, Marissa, and the small yet stately home that had belonged to Papa Dee.

She parked the golf cart next to another that sat in the driveway along with a Boss Construction company truck and an SUV. Knowing Jackson was out and Diamond was resting, she opened the unlocked door and walked inside.

"Diamond?"

"In here!"

London followed her cousin's voice down a long hall to a room with windows for walls. From here one could see almost the entire vineyard, from the rolling hills of grapevines to the stable of horses, the sparkling pond for fishing and both the Temescal and Santa Ana mountain ranges. You couldn't see the hotel, wine store or executive offices, as per Diamond's specific instructions. She'd told Jackson she did not want to bring work into her house.

Diamond lay sprawled on a chaise in a canary yellow baby doll mini, looking big-belly beautiful with cantaloupes for breasts. "About time you got here. With Faye ordering me to come lie down, you're today's entertainment. I don't much appreciate you making me wait."

"Stop being divalicious. Your sister-in-law played the doctor card, as she well should, and Aunt Genevieve eyed my every move. Your decorum-conscious mama wasn't going to let me leave early, especially since I'd arrived so—"

"Yes, whatever. Enough about that. Let's get to the reason you were tardy. Ace Montgomery and your bribing Ellen—my employee, by the way—to give his massage."

London waved away Diamond's stern segue. "Don't worry about that."

"Don't brush me off."

"Calm down, girl, before you bring on contractions."

"I'm serious, London. You bribed an employee into breaking a company rule. We could have been sued! Any other instance and she would have been fired. But Ellen is a hard worker with a stellar record whose family has experienced a year of financial setbacks. Five thousand dollars cash was understandably hard to pass up. Plus, I know how tenacious you can be."

"I'm sorry, Diamond. I guess I didn't look at it from a corporate angle."

"Obviously."

"Please tell me she's not fired."

"No, but she was written up and put on a ninety-day probation. If there are no more incidents, after a year we'll remove it from her file."

"I really am sorry, cousin. Forgive me?"

"I'll think about it." The frown lines disappeared as Diamond relaxed. "So tell me the who, what, when, where and why of it all. I want to hear everything."

London obliged, relating everything from overhearing the girls in the bathroom to Ace's take-charge ways. "I let him get away with it this time. I bribed my way into his room and all. But next time he tries to boss me around, no matter the situation, I'm going to put him in check."

"Careful with that. I'm married to an alpha male. Trying to put them in check is a pretty tall order that usually ends with them on top. In fact, I think it was just such a conversation that led to my stomach now looking like this."

"Well, I'm not going to let a man boss me around." London looked at her watch and abruptly stood. "Time is flying! I've got to run. Ace and I are having dinner at eight. He said if I were late there'd be consequences." She rushed over to Diamond for a quick hug and kiss and hurried out the room. "Bye!"

As London reached the end of the hall and headed toward the door, she heard Diamond burst out laughing.

Chapter 5

"You're late."

London took a step back from the bungalow's front door. "That is not a proper greeting."

Six feet of I-don't-give-a-damn filled the large frame and looked amazing in the process.

Had she read minds, Ace thought, she would have known his brusque behavior covered up how much her beauty threw him off guard. "I apologize. Good evening, London. You're late."

London rewarded him with a smile. "I'm sorry," she whispered, leaning in to give him a feathery kiss on the cheek. Her eyes were wide and pleading. "Forgive me?" She nibbled her lip, awaiting his response.

He placed his hand on her shoulder, slid it to the nape of her neck and placed soft, plump lips on her forehead. "I forgive you."

He stepped back so she could enter. "I just won't be able to give you the gift I purchased earlier today."

A lover of presents no matter the reason, London unleashed her inner child. She whirled around, eyes shining. "What'd you get me?"

"Nothing now. We talked about your tardiness already. You obviously didn't feel my time was important." He reached into an inside jacket pocket and pulled out a small gift-wrapped box. "Please, have a seat and excuse me for a sec while I put this away."

"Ace!" London, fast on his heels, tried to reach around him and grab the box.

He turned and blocked her. "What are you doing?" His eyes shined with humor.

"Trying to get what belongs to me!"

London was five foot eight so it wasn't easy, but Ace being four inches taller helped him keep the box out of her reach.

"When one doesn't follow the rules, there are consequences. I told you that." He took his eyes on a slow journey down her body. "But you're irresistible. So here."

London beamed. "Thank you, Ace! What is it?"

"Open it and find out."

She dropped her purse on the coffee table and sat on the couch where they'd conversed earlier. After another sexy look at him, she lifted the lid on the bow-wrapped gift and opened the leather box inside.

"Wow, this is beautiful!" London lifted from the case a platinum wine stopper topped with Swarovski crystals in the shape of a large grape. "You got this in the gift shop?"

"It's not available there. This is something that was created for the Drake companies' largest buyers and A-list clients, a very limited-edition piece."

"Wait! They're my family. How'd you get on the inside for a limited edition?"

"I have skills."

London's eyes glided from the wine stopper to Ace's face. "That you do."

Three words, but they cut through the easy banter and casual chitchat to what was on both of their minds. That weekend in London. Literally and figuratively.

"I have something else for you."

London eyed him up and down. "I'm ready."

Ace chuckled, flattered and flummoxed at the same time. "Dinner will be here in ten minutes. Would you like an aperitif?"

"Sure."

Ace walked through the dining room into the kitchen. London followed him, taking in the sophisticated charm of the two-bedroom bungalow with its formal dining room and a stunning galley kitchen that featured brick backsplashes, copper counters and black stainless steel appliances.

"I still can't believe you're here, at my cousin's resort."

"And I can't believe you're here, in my bungalow. I chose this place specifically because of the privacy it afforded."

"Guess our meeting was meant to be."

She watched as Ace pulled a beautiful bottle from a shiny square box. The frosted glass sparkled in the dim lighting, and while it wasn't as beautiful as the wine stopper Ace had given her, the top on the bottle was a luxurious design.

"What's that?"

"Another limited edition. This is Drake Wines's newest creation. It hasn't even been released."

"Okay, which of my cousins do you know? It has to be family giving you this type of access."

"Dexter. When you got called back to your family, I went on a tour of the winery. He was my guide. I told him we were meeting for dinner. He thought we'd enjoy his latest creation."

"Dexter is good people. I can see you two getting along."

"Absolutely. He likes my clothes."

"I can see that." Ace reached for two goblets from a glass-front cabinet. "This is wild, man. I can't believe you're here."

"Ditto. It's been, what, three or four years since we've seen each other?"

"More like five. That's how long I've been away from modeling full-time."

"What happened? One minute you were on top of the modeling world and the next minute you'd quit and gone to college? And what made you decide to become a designer? Had that always been your plan? How'd you even know what to do? I have so many questions."

The brass door knocker sounded. "That's our dinner." He moved to walk by her. "I have questions, too. Before the night is over, we both might get answers to them all."

Normally the waitstaff stayed and served the meals brought to the bungalows. But Ace and London wanted privacy. After the young man had set the table, placed the entrées in a warming oven and served the appetizer, Ace tipped the grateful waiter and sent him on his way. The lights had been dimmed. Tapered candles in glass bowls at the table's center sent shadows dancing against the silk walls. The flowers in tall corner vases were gorgeous and real. The aroma from the warming food wafted into the room. Ace reentered, too. He stopped in the doorway, watching London study the painting that had caught his attention earlier.

"Pretty cool, huh?"

"Yes. I think I've met this painter. Funny that his work would be on display here."

He picked up their goblets and handed one to her when he reached her side. "I say we toast to coincidence."

London laughed as they clinked glasses. "Cheers."

"Let me get your chair."

"Thank you."

They sat, Ace at the head, London beside him. "You look beautiful tonight. Did I tell you that?"

"No. You were too busy berating me for being late."

"Ha! I was messing with you mostly—got to keep a woman like you on your toes. I like your perfume, too. It's actually the first thing I recognized when you came over this afternoon. I knew Ellen hadn't been wearing that scent but explained it away in my head. I still can't believe you did that when a phone call would have sufficed."

"As I said earlier, I didn't want to give you the chance to turn me down. The thought came into my head when I overheard the workers, and I just went with it." London bit into the toasted focaccia bread placed atop a spicy tomato bisque. "I think surprising you in person was more exciting than a phone call, don't you?"

Ace dug in to the appetizer, as well. "*Exciting* wouldn't be my first word choice."

"What would?"

"Shocking. Scary."

"You don't mean that."

"Yes, I do. That was pretty bold, what you did today. And a little rude."

This comment surprised her. "Rude? How?"

"Do I really have to explain how that was an invasion of privacy?"

"I assumed you'd want your privacy invaded," she

mumbled. "Diamond was mad at me, too." She sat back, dejected. "It's stuff like this that got me sent away in the first place."

"I don't mean to make you feel bad."

"I can leave if you want."

"If I'd wanted that, I wouldn't have invited you to dinner." He studied London's troubled expression. The pain he saw there troubled him, too.

"Where were you sent away from?"

He watched as she shook off the melancholy and donned a nonchalant air. "Let's just say going to school in Europe wasn't my idea." She looked at him then offered a sincere smile. "It's a long story. Maybe some other time."

"Is that your subtle way of trying to ensure another date?"

"I'm the bold, rude ingrate who crashed your massage, remember? There are many words that could be used to describe me. *Subtle* isn't one of them."

The honest answer touched Ace's heart and awakened an unexplainable desire to protect her. He quickly squashed the notion. A woman like her didn't need a man like him. Her company was refreshing, though. He soon realized what made being with her different. He was enjoying himself, feeling relaxed and complete, and he tried to remember the last time he'd felt this way. It had been a while.

"There isn't a woman here. Surprising for the Ace I remember. What's up with that?"

While he'd come here to get away from work, Ace welcomed the change of subject. "Right now my woman is a new line being unveiled at fashion week."

"Next month? In New York?" Ace nodded. "What's the line?"

"It's a secret." London fixed her mouth in a pout. Sexy, luscious, but Ace didn't budge. "You know how the industry works. It's all about the big reveal." He paused for a drink of water, gazed at her over the rim as he drank. "I really want to tell you, though. Maybe I will soon."

"If not, I'll just make sure to attend your show."

"How many shows are you doing?"

"I don't know yet. I hadn't planned to do any, but… those plans have changed."

"Because of your breakup with Max?"

"Partly. We were supposed to be filming his movie right now. But it's also to take a break. I've lived overseas for years and promised my parents I'd spend time with them."

"Coming on to me the way you have makes it seem you've gotten over him. But that could be an act, like your being hurt when I didn't call you back. Are you okay?"

"Max didn't want to let go, but I'm okay." London finished her soup and reached for the chilled Chardonnay the waiter had poured them. She took a thoughtful sip. "And just for the record, I was hurt that you didn't call me back. A little bit."

"You had plenty of guys lined up behind me. Wasn't there even a stalker for a while?"

Now it was London's turn to be surprised. "How'd you know about that?"

"Insider information. You know we run in the same circles, or used to."

"My people signed confidentiality agreements regarding this. We didn't want it leaked to the public and give some other troubled soul ideas. So who told you?"

"It was Trent Corrigan. He told me in confidence and I haven't shared it further."

"Quinn's best friend. She's one of my sisters-in-law."

"So it was true."

"Unfortunately, yes. A guy I'd met casually while living in Paris. He interviewed me for his website. That's how he got my number. After a series of interviews, he asked me out. When I declined he got crazy. I got a restraining order. He violated it several times before they finally put him in jail."

"That had to be scary."

"At first it was just annoying. But when he followed me back here to the States…"

"He came over here?"

"Right up to my hotel room door in New York City."

"That's insane. It's a wonder you don't walk around with bodyguards."

"For a while I did. Guards named Terrell, Niko, Warren and Ike, otherwise known as my older brothers."

Ace laughed. "How'd that go?"

"It didn't last long. They wanted me to hide out in Paradise Cove, my hometown, but I refused to live in fear. With him in jail, I went back to Paris, where I lived at the time. Thankfully they have lives, wives and careers, and couldn't follow me. Until then, I was shielded by a wall of Drakes.

"Has that ever happened to you? The whole stalker thing?"

"Yes, but not to the same extent as it did to you. My stalkers got the message before law enforcement had to be involved."

"*Stalkers* plural, huh? I'm not surprised."

Ace was. Not at her comments, but at the feelings bubbling in his heart for the woman he now drank in with his eyes.

"Why do you keep staring at me?"

"You should be used to people staring at you. Ready for the entrée?"

"I'm starving for it." Though the pecan-crusted lemon swordfish smelled heavenly, the look she gave suggested her comment was not about that at all. Ace understood. He felt the same way. But he couldn't give in to the desire for physical pleasure. Not now that he'd decided she was the one, the perfect model to anchor the OTB Her line. He'd conduct himself professionally. This was about business. Or so he told himself. Time would tell.

Chapter 6

He wasn't expected back until Tuesday, but Ace strolled into his office on Monday morning at eight o'clock sharp, motivated, excited and ready to work. Seeing London had brought all his thoughts about the runway show together around a cohesive concept and had inspired an idea for a showstopping final piece. He now knew exactly the type of woman the new line represented. He'd spent the day with her. London was his muse.

After a trip to the break room to fortify himself with a cup of java, Ace returned to the office, rolled up his designer shirtsleeves and pulled out a sketch pad. The pencil fairly flew across the paper as lines, swirls and varied strokes brought Ace's vision to life. The sketch was detailed and specific. Lucien, the TV design show winner who'd sent in his portfolio just last week, would have no problem bringing his vision to life. Ace was sure of it.

"What the heck are you doing here?"

Immersed in sketching the intricate design he envisioned on the stand-up collar of the London-Clarisse trench coat–inspired finale design, Ace hadn't heard Tyler come down the hall or enter his office.

"Dent! My man!" Ace rubbed his palms together like an excited young boy. "Have a seat."

Tyler eyed Ace with skepticism as he sat down. The toned, tan blond with mystical gray eyes and a dimpled smile was the company's CFO and Ace's good friend for the past five years.

"You aren't due back until tomorrow."

"I know, but I couldn't wait. I found the star model for our runway shows. Or rather, she found me. And you're not going to believe who it is."

"The way your eyes are shining I'd say either Mariah, Rihanna or Michelle Obama."

"Close. London."

Tyler's eyes narrowed. "Frida said you were at a vineyard near San Diego."

Frida was Ace's executive assistant, named after the talented, outspoken Mexican artist, and she was equally unreserved.

"I was."

"But working, obviously, instead of taking our advice to do anything but that. Thanks for the email on Lucien, though. He's definitely our guy."

"You're welcome. But I actually met her while doing exactly what you guys suggested."

"London was at the vineyard?"

"Her family owns it."

"Get the hell out of here. Are we talking about the same London, the gorgeous international supermodel and the darling of Europe?" Ace nodded. "Her family lives in… What's the name of the town?"

"Temecula."

"Her family lives there?"

"Her first cousins do."

"And London just happened to be there visiting them. Why don't I believe this?"

"If the tables were turned, I wouldn't, either. But she was there. Our meeting was coincidental."

Ace told Tyler about London's relative Papa Dee and why the family had been there last weekend. "The moment I saw her," he finished, "I knew she was the one to bring this line to life, to make it the hit we want it to be and so much more. Get her on our runway and we'll be all everyone is talking about from New York to Paris and from London to Milan."

"What did she say about booking her?"

"I didn't ask."

This elicited the famous Dent scowl Tyler's family was known for. "Have you forgotten that fashion week is a month away? She's probably already booked up. Breaking up with Max Tata has made her even more popular than when she was dating him. We'll be lucky if we can get her."

"We'll do everything it takes to make that happen. I want to pull out all the stops."

"Why didn't you just ask her yourself?"

"I did, indirectly. Not about working our runway but about whether or not she was totally booked. She isn't. But there were other reasons. I didn't want to make a decision based off a gut—*or loin*—reaction to seeing her so unexpectedly. London is one of the most beautiful women on the planet. Period. But everyone in the industry knows she can be temperamental and scandalous. Plus, she commands a hefty fee. We need to weigh the pros against the cons."

"When it comes to cons, I don't see any. The world loves controversy. If London makes headlines, let's just hope she does so while wearing OTB."

"I hate to agree with that callous observation."

"But you know it's true."

"Unfortunately, yes." Ace had unwittingly caused a scandal or two himself. Like dating a thirty-three-year-old top model when he was just nineteen. Or getting trapped inside an Atlanta hotel room after someone leaked his room number and dozens of women showed up outside his door—some in their underwear. Hotel security had been overwhelmed. Police had to be called. One woman was arrested for indecent exposure. The media had eaten it up.

"Booking London is a no-brainer. What were your other reasons?"

Ace hesitated. He'd told no one about the weekend he'd spent with London years ago. No one but the two of them knew they'd shared those lascivious forty-eight hours. Only Ace knew that the torch he'd once carried for her had burned very brightly. He planned to keep it that way. And he intended to keep his distance from her. His heart was still raw from betrayal. He was older now. Established and thinking of settling down. If that fire got stoked again, making her his exclusively was just about the only way he could see putting it out. This past weekend she'd made it clear that marriage was not on her mind.

"Booking her is a matter for Mira to handle, not me. I want London's agent contacted the moment Mira arrives."

Mira Jacobs was the company's tough-as-nails attorney who handled OTB's legal matters and also oversaw the company's brand.

Tyler pulled out his phone. "I'll text her now, find out when she's planning to come in."

While Tyler texted Mira, Ace took a photo of what he'd sketched and sent it to Lucien along with the message, Let's talk.

Tyler placed his phone on the desk. "Now let's discuss what's really important."

"I can't think of anything more important right now than fashion week, but...go ahead?"

"Did you hit it?"

Ace's look? Deadpan.

"Don't give me that look as if I asked something crazy. She's a beautiful woman. There's no way I'd have passed up the chance for some of that!" A beat and then Tyler finished, "If I weren't as gay as the earth is round."

"Can't say I didn't think about it. What red-blooded man wouldn't? But right through here I'm all about business. Getting this line ready should be the only thing on our minds."

The day passed quickly. Shortly after Tyler left Ace's office, Lucien arrived, excited about and impressed with the design Ace had texted him. Ace spoke with Mira about London and then called a meeting with the designers to implement his latest ideas. More changes were made to the fall menswear line that they would be showing this spring, and the direction of the OTB Her line was clarified and expanded. After a phone powwow with finance, the PR and marketing budgets were increased. The partners decided not to reveal the news about London until it was a done deal, but in regard to the design team, he'd let it be known that a famous face would be among the models wearing the clothing.

Speculation ran rampant. Ace didn't mind. Nothing like a bit of healthy competition among the models to bring out everyone's A game. Throughout the day, his cell phone was nearby. Now that everyone was on board with London as the fashion show's star model, he wanted to get the contract signed and make it official. Five o'clock came and went, and then six. He contacted Mira. There was still no word. He turned off his office lights and left the building just before seven without an answer. As he entered his driveway around seven thirty, his phone rang. The number showed up unknown, a common occurrence on his company phone. He pressed the answer button on the steering wheel, and heard a familiar voice.

"So… Ace Montgomery… I hear you want my body after all."

Chapter 7

London looked at the phone, cold and silent in her hand. *He hung up on me?* The thought barely finished before her ringtone sounded. The words of her favorite song— Jan Baker's "Who I Am"—blasted from the speaker, the words *OTB Fashion* showed on her screen.

"For someone wanting my services, that was not a good move."

Ace chuckled, a low, sexy sound that made London's kitty purr.

"I apologize. I'd just gotten home, and when I turned off the car my phone didn't switch over. It normally does."

"I guess I'll forgive you…this time."

"I'd appreciate it."

"Is it true? You want my body?"

"Yes."

A pause, pregnant with possibilities and promises, followed his response.

"Then why were you acting all reserved in Temecula? I could have easily been your dessert last night."

"I was speaking professionally. Our new line was designed with women like you in mind. My partners and I would very much like to make you the star model in the OTB Her fashion show."

"So that's the big secret you couldn't share the other day. OTB is introducing a women's line."

"Not just a women's line, but the embodiment of a woman's attitude. It's been in development for a while, a couple years, really, since its conception. But in being around you, I saw all the pieces come together. You embody the woman these clothes are designed for. When I suggested to my partners that you might not be booked up for fashion week, they couldn't get to your agent fast enough."

"Now I understand the gift of the flower."

"What flower?"

"That stunning single Kinabalu orchid, and in a Baccarat vase, no less. Classy move, Mr. Montgomery. It doesn't happen easily, but I'm impressed."

"Wow. I'm tempted to keep my mouth shut and take the credit. But when the real person came forward I'd look like a dishonest fool."

"You didn't send the flower?" Discomfort replaced intrigue.

"No, London, I didn't. Where was it delivered?"

"The hotel's front desk. I called the bungalow, but you'd checked out already."

"You must have made quite an impression on another hotel guest."

"No. I stayed in one of my family's private guesthouses. Was only in the hotel a couple times and tried to stay incognito. One guy recognized me, though. We took a selfie. Oh, well. I'll call the hotel later and see what information I can get from them. Right now—" the flirty tone returned "—I'm trying to see what I can get from you."

"You are a very tempting morsel, London. Even all these years later, I remember those nights we shared. But I'm no longer that promiscuous, impulsive man you met in London, the one for whom having sex was as common as eating lunch, and indulged in almost as often. These days, for me, it's not so much about having sex as it is about making love."

"So who is she?"

"Who?"

"The lucky woman who's getting that love. And don't tell me you're celibate, because there is no way I'd believe you."

"No, I'm not celibate. But I'm also no longer into casual sex. I don't judge those who are—each to his own. But as I told you yesterday, my love affair has been with the secret you now know about… OTB Her. In one way or another, that's how I've been spending my nights and weekends. My partners ordered me to Temecula for vacation. They were right. I was stressed the hell out. But now I know the real reason I ended up there. It was so I could run into you."

"So we could do business together. This is all about business, nothing more?"

"Right now, that's all I'm about, period. Plus, I'm not sure I could keep it casual with you. And I'm equally unclear if I could handle a relationship right now."

"Sounds like there's a story there. You know about me and Max. It's only fair I get under your sheets, one way or another."

"You're right. There's a story. Maybe one day. Right

now, though, the story I'm trying to do with you is one that will rock the runways this fashion season and then rock the world. Don't make a decision right now. Just take a meeting with us. We'll handle everything. Once you see what we've designed for the ladies, you'll be in. Guaranteed."

"You're that sure of yourself, huh?"

"No, but it sounded good."

"Ha! Indeed. Let me think about it and get back to you."

"When? I don't mean to rush you, but New York Fashion Week is next month."

"I won't take long."

"Thank you, London. I look forward to seeing you later this week."

"Stop sounding so sexy before I demand a rider to any contract I sign with OTB...you."

London hung up and went to the sitting room of the west-wing suite in her parents' Paradise Cove estate. It was where her older sister, Teresa, had lived before marrying Atka, her Alaskan love. She walked around the room, idly picked up porcelain and crystal knickknacks, and replayed Ace's offer in her head. Truth of the matter was, she didn't need to think about it. She'd already accepted it mentally before the words had fully left his mouth. No need for him to know that, though. Whenever possible, it was always best to let a man sweat. In truth, that's what she really wanted—Ace's sheen-covered body hovering over her own. He was sexy and by far the best lover she'd ever had. But even that wasn't his main attraction. What made him most irresistible was that he'd turned her down. For London, it was a first. And a challenge. Drakes lived for challenges. And they didn't like the word *no*.

Her phone chirped, indicating a message. London returned to her bedroom, hoping it was Ace having changed his mind about their hooking up. But it was her agent, with yet another booking opportunity. She'd told the agency she was sitting out this fashion season. Now that she was contemplating walking for OTB, her agent had decided to field other calls. The phone hadn't stopped ringing. Instead of calling Incomparable, London rang Quinn. That Ace hadn't sent the flower bothered her more than she wanted to admit. She got voice mail, left a message and then went downstairs.

She found her parents, Ike Sr. and Jennifer, in their favorite sitting room. Her father slowly swirled a tumbler of brandy. Jennifer drank tea.

"Hey, you two."

"Hello, dear," Jennifer replied.

"Evening, Clarisse," Ike said, eyeing her warily over his tumbler.

London didn't bother correcting her father. To her parents, she'd always be Clarisse. She walked over to an ornate buffet crafted of ebony wood and poured a glass of sparkling water.

"Are you joining us for dinner, dear?"

"Yes. What's for dinner?"

"Oh, no, you must want something. Let me lock away my checkbook."

"Now, Ike. Don't tease like that. Sweetie, is everything all right?"

"Everything's fine, Mom." Except for the expensive gift from a stranger. That didn't feel fine at all. But why share and have three people worried? "Don't worry, Dad. Thanks to your suggestion years ago to hire a financial planner, my bank accounts and investment portfolios are all very healthy. Your checkbook is safe from me."

Ike nodded. "Good."

"I do have a question to ask, though, and a potential favor."

"I knew it!" Ike shook his head sadly. "You were such a quiet, obedient child. But since hitting the teen years you've caused ninety of the one hundred gray hairs I now have on my head."

"Ike Drake! That is simply not true. If I recall correctly it's seventy-five."

"Thanks, Mom."

"We want to renovate the west-wing suite for her to live. And here you are, pushing her away. We're very proud of you, Clarisse. And we're so glad you're home. Would you like something besides water? Wine or tea?"

"I'm fine."

"Then let's move to the dining room."

The three bypassed the larger dining room and the table for twelve and continued to the smaller table off the family room.

"Just us tonight?" London asked.

"Yes," Ike answered, "and that's fine with me. I saw enough Drakes this past weekend to last me till summer."

"Mr. Drake. You're being a rascal. What has gotten into you tonight?"

"Didn't say I didn't love them. Just that I don't need to see so many again until the next reunion."

The three sat down to a light dinner prepared by the chef. After small talk about the weekend, Ike shifted the conversation.

"Tell me about this favor."

"I might need to go to San Francisco this week and wanted to know if the plane was available."

Ike raised a brow. "The company plane?"

"Unless you've purchased one for recreational use, yes, Dad, that's the one."

Jennifer chuckled.

"That plane is to be used for company business only."

"This is business."

"Drake Realty Plus business?"

"In a way. My last name is Drake."

Both her parents laughed at that.

"San Francisco is less than two hours away, honey," Jennifer said.

"You know I don't drive."

Ike's fork stopped midair. "Doesn't mean you can't. Or you can hire a driver."

Jennifer reached for the linen napkin beside her plate, wiped her mouth and turned to her daughter. "What's happening in San Francisco?"

London told them about seeing Ace in Temecula and about his modeling offer.

Jennifer's eyes brightened. "I know about that young man."

"You remember his underwear ads, Mom?"

Ike looked at his wife. "Careful with your answer, hon."

Jennifer's eyes sparkled as she looked at Ike. "Honey, the only underwear that has caught my eye for the past thirty years has been worn by you."

"Oh, Lord." London groaned, but secretly she enjoyed seeing her parents interact this way. They'd given her the perfect vision of what true love looked like. "How'd you hear about Ace?"

"A couple weeks ago, at a meeting with the fund-raising committee. In fact, I was planning to talk about it with you and ask you to participate. It's for the community center. We're planning a charity fashion show event featuring local designers and models, as well. OTB Him is one of the companies we reached out to."

"Did you hear anything yet?"

"No. The letters went out just last week."

"I thought you were taking a break from modeling," Ike said. "Making a point to spend more time with your family."

"The big one you don't need to see anymore until next year?"

"Don't get cute, young lady. I'm talking about your immediate family. Your grandparents are getting older. You owe them a visit. You've got nieces and nephews you barely know, and in-laws, too."

"Whose fault is that?" London mumbled.

"You really want my answer?" Ike challenged.

"Let's not go there, you two. The past is over and can't be retrieved. Let's treat the present like it is, a gift."

It had always been this way between London and her father. The friction came from the fact they were so much alike.

"I do want to stay close by, Dad," London admitted. "Being with the family this weekend made me realize how much I've truly missed you guys, how I've just missed…family. And while I'm sure this will shock the both of you I really am ready to take a break from my jet-setter life. I'm taking off from full-time modeling for at least a year. This job would be for a month, basically walking the four major fashion weeks for OTB, and that's it."

Jennifer nodded. "New York, Paris, Milan…and what's the other?"

"Really, Mom?"

"Oh, right!" Jennifer laughed. "London!" She placed a hand on Ike's forearm. "Perhaps one of the executives has business up north, darling," Jennifer offered. "I recall you mentioning Junior having a meeting at Ten Drake Plaza. Clarisse can ride along and see our latest acquisition. Getting a designer like Mr. Montgomery on board could mean lots of money for the community center."

"Yes, Dad," London added, "the Drake Community Center. Company business."

"Where are my sons when I need them? I'm clearly outnumbered." Ike's look toward his daughter was one of exasperation mixed with a grudging respect. "Ike has a meeting at Ten Drake Plaza on Wednesday or Thursday. You can ride up with him. But for the return? You're on your own. It won't kill you to fly commercial."

"Thanks, Dad!" London kissed her father's cheek and headed toward the hallway.

"Clarisse, where are you going?"

"To call my agent to make the appointment with Ace."

"In the middle of dinner?"

"It will just take a moment. I'll be back before my food gets cold."

London took the stairs two at a time. She was a veteran, had performed in amazing runway shows all over the world. But none had felt quite as exciting as this one. Because if London had her way, she'd walk directly off that runway into Ace Montgomery's bedroom.

Chapter 8

The next day a knock sounded on Ace's office door. It opened before he could say a word.

"By all means, Mira, come on in."

She did—smiling wide, eyes beaming. "I've got great news and an even greater idea." She sat in one of two chairs facing Ace's paper-strewn desk. "London's agent just called. She's in."

Ace nodded, still absorbed in the designs on his computer screen.

"Ace, did you hear me?"

"Yes. London has agreed to meet with us. I knew she might."

"No, not just meet with us. She's agreed to walk the runway in all four shows!"

Ace slowly raised his head. "Are you sure?"

"I know, it's amazing. I can't believe she's available. And believe it or not, her fee is such that once the shows are over, we'll still have money in the bank."

Ace sat back, searching for meaning behind London's quick and affirmative answer. "That is great news."

"I thought you'd be more excited."

"I am. Just stunned. I mean, I talked to her, but—"

"You've talked to her?" He nodded. "How cozy."

"No big deal. We exchanged numbers in Temecula. She'll be amazing."

"Is there something I need to know about you two?"

"Nope. Nada."

"Because as the person overseeing marketing and branding, a romantic liaison happening between an owner and a celebrity model repping the line is something I'd rather learn from you instead of a tabloid."

"There's nothing going on, Mira."

"Has there ever been? I'm asking that not as the company rep but as a nosy peer."

Ace smiled. "London and I traveled in the same circles, and our paths crossed a time or two—parties, shows, stuff like that. But we were both so busy then—she was the star of Incomparable and I was the face of Noire Underwear. Before our chance meeting in Temecula, I hadn't seen her in years."

"If I have my way, you'll be seeing her a lot more. We all will."

"You've got my attention."

"I think we should make London more than just our star model for fashion week. I think we should make her the face of OTB Her."

Ace's response was immediate. "Okay, whoa. Having her star in our shows is one thing. But an ongoing relationship? I'm not sure that's such a good idea."

"It's a great idea. A fantastic one! We'll be lucky to get her, and if we do, she'd make an amazing spokesperson for OTB Her. She's young, gorgeous, successful and popular. The paparazzi are always trying to get a shot of her. The tabloids and celebrity websites adore her. We should be so lucky that she'd agree to represent us. Now—" Mira leaned forward and looked Ace straight in the eye "—give me one reason why I'm wrong."

"Okay. You've got me. I can't think of any."

None that he could voice, anyway. All he knew was that his life had just gotten complicated. Because there was no way he and London could be around each other on a regular basis and ignore the sexual energy between them. She'd made her intentions clear. He'd held back, but wanted her just as much. The attraction was too strong, the physical compatibility undeniable. The question wasn't if, but when. And how to involve his body while protecting his heart.

"I've scheduled a meeting for this Thursday. Her agent and publicist will be joining us. I also think it would be a good idea for us to have some of the clothes ready, even if only the muslin mock-ups."

"Agreed. I'll have Lucien get on the final piece right away, to see if what we've envisioned can actually work."

"It's not an original idea, but I haven't seen it done quite the way you've planned. If we can pull that off... Wow!"

"Hey, what's all the excitement about in here?" Tyler walked in wearing a suede OTB suit, looking like a model himself.

"We got London," Mira answered.

"Yes!"

"And she's going to be the face of the line."

"Damn right!"

"Slow down, you two. She's said yes to walking the shows, nothing more."

"Don't worry about that," Tyler replied smugly. "Just

pour on the charm, Ace, do what you do. She'll say yes to it all."

Ace simply nodded and looked away. Her saying yes to everything both frightened and excited him at the same time.

Had anyone pointed it out, he would have disagreed, but as Ace arose on Thursday morning he took special pains with his appearance. Since he'd gotten a facial and a manicure the day before, his clean-shaven cocoa skin was smooth to the touch and blemish free. The black silk OTB suit with leather embellishments showed off his six-foot frame to perfection. The open-collar tan shirt he wore beneath it both complemented his skin and highlighted the signature color of the OTB Her line. The gold jewelry was a perfect finish, along with his Burberry wing tips. Someone on the outside looking in might have thought it was Ace going for a position and not the other way around.

His extra sharp appearance didn't go without notice. Mira was in the break room when he entered for coffee. She took a step back, and then another. "Dressed to impress, I see. Very nice, Mr. CEO."

Tyler passed him in the executive hallways and offered a knowing smile. "I see you're pulling out all the stops to win over our client. My man!"

Ace blew them both off. They were right. But he didn't need to tell them.

The day passed quickly. Everyone prepared for the afternoon's meeting. Just before she headed home, Frida walked into his office. "They're here, Ace. Tyler is already in the conference room."

"Make sure they're comfortable. I'm on my way."

Frida nodded and left. Ace looked at his watch. Four thirty exactly. London, on time? He stood, a slightly smug smile on his face as he buttoned his jacket and reached for his tablet and phone. If she kept offering nice surprises like this, their partnership might go better than he imagined.

London admired everything about OTB's offices. The decor was sleek and classy, just like its owner. She couldn't remember the last time she'd been nervous at a meeting. If she ever had. But there were little butterflies fluttering around her stomach. When Ace entered—no, sauntered, strolled, ambled into—the room, the butterflies took off flying, causing other areas of her body to flutter, as well.

"Good afternoon," he said as he walked over to give a handshake and cheek kiss to London's agent and publicist.

"And to you, London, the star of the OTB runway." He leaned down for a hug. "Thanks so much for coming and for agreeing to represent our new line."

He smelled like daring and machismo and good lovemaking. His body was hard, his hug nice and firm. She took in his perfectly coordinated look. They could have done a photo shoot on the spot. Her off-the-shoulder tan mini with faux-fur trim was the exact same color as his shirt. She too wore gold jewelry laced with black onyx, tying together her ensemble with her black Taylor Plateau pumps. Her hair had been pulled back in a high ponytail to expose her flawless skin, high cheekbones and long neck. She'd considered showing up in jeans and a tee. She was glad her agent had changed her mind.

London watched as Ace walked to the front of the conference room. He was poised and commanding, looking every inch the company exec. She saw him in a new light. The brightness looked good on him.

"Again, thank you all for coming. I know everyone's

time is valuable, so we'll get started right away. London, on behalf of my partners, Tyler Dent and Mira Jacobs, we couldn't be more excited about you joining us for these upcoming shows. You'll rock these looks and ensure that during the course of these shows all over the world, OTB Her is all everyone is talking about. The head of our design team, Lucien, has put together a video presentation of the new line and has also created muslin mock-ups for the featured pieces. So, without further ado, I present OTB... Her."

Ace connected his tablet to a wall projector outlet. With the push of a button near him, the room lights dimmed. The projector started and into the room burst picture after picture of bold, unique looks done in various shades of tan, accessorized with bright primary colors. Few comments were made as two dozen images were cast against the projector wall. But when the final piece was revealed, the room was filled with a collective gasp—London's among them.

The end of the presentation was met with applause. The room brightened once again. There were smiles all around.

"Ace, you've outdone yourself. That last piece is stunning...more than that, really. I have no words. The way it's designed, though, with all of that crinoline and the funky train, it will be a beast to walk in and looks to work better on someone seven feet tall."

"Which brings me to my next question," Ace calmly countered. "Can you walk in stilts?"

London's look to her agent read, *are you kidding?* Then she voiced the question.

Ace met her skepticism with laughter. "Totally appropriate response, but hear us out. We have someone designing a special set of eighteen-inch stilts that will take us head and shoulders above the competition, literally. All our models will wear them. That finale piece that you raved about will require stilts two and a half feet tall. I think you can handle it, London. And be the talk of the town."

They discussed specifics about the line. London agreed to try the stilts. Once all the questions about the runway shows had been answered, Ace had just one more question.

"You've agreed to be our star model for fashion week, but we want more." His pregnant pause was enough to birth a love affair. "We want to offer you the job as spokeswoman for and face of OTB Her. Is that something you'd want and think you could handle?"

For a second he and London were the only ones in the room. Oh, yes, she could handle that and much, much more. But again she held her cards close to the chest with four of her favorite words.

"I'll think about it."

Chapter 9

Later that evening, everyone from the meeting joined a couple investors at a trendy seafood restaurant located near San Francisco's affluent Nob Hill. Ace ordered a bottle of their best champagne. Once flutes had been filled, he lifted his up.

"To London, the supermodel and superwoman who will bring OTB Her...out of the box."

"Hear, hear!"

"Cheers!"

"Yes!"

"Absolutely!"

Responses mingled with the clinking of crystal before everyone took a sip of the pricey bubbly.

Michael Watson, a hip-hop artist from Oakland known to the world as 100 Proof, who'd been diversifying his $100 million portfolio into real estate, restaurants and more, sat back and gazed at London. "I see you brought the fire," he said to Ace, his eyes still on her. "I was about eighty percent sure I'd invest when it was just the men's line. But now you've got one for the ladies? Starring this one right here? It's a game changer, brother. Count me all the way in."

"Good to hear," Ace replied with a slight smile that London observed didn't quite reach his eyes. When Michael reached over for London's hand, she saw Ace's jaw clench and release, even though he maintained his smile.

"We're hoping all three of you will come on board," Mira said. "And quickly. We were going to try and keep OTB Her under wraps until the show, but the publicity division feels it better to leak the information and create a buzz and a mystery around the woman wearing the clothes. We'll be doing photo shoots as early as next week, and throughout the season. It's too late for print magazines, but we plan to have a heavy presence on fashion websites, blogs and billboards and buildings in Times Square. With all three of you investing, we could do much more."

The other two investors—one a former football player, the other a Silicon Valley executive's wife—took a little more time to convince. But after two hours and a steady stream of some of the best seafood in the Pacific Ocean— roasted mussels, Dungeness crab, pan-seared sea bass and cioppino, the seafood stew that originated in the city by the bay, along with thin slices of Wagyu filet mignon— and London's effortless banter about time spent traipsing her European playground, the investors were putty in her hands and their money was headed toward OTB's coffers.

Outside the restaurant, the group said their goodbyes. Ace was standing on London's left side. Michael, Mr. 100 Proof, sidled up to her right. "Hey, London, I know a spot over near the financial district, a private club owned by a friend of mine. Why don't you come hang out with me and, you know, let me show you off a little bit?"

London sensed more than felt Ace stiffen beside her. "Thank you, but I have another engagement. In fact—" she looked at her watch "—I really should be going."

Michael looked her up and down. "As fine as you are, we've got to hang out."

"Thanks, Michael. I'll be pretty busy between now and New York Fashion Week."

"In New York, then. I'm a patient man."

Ace gently squeezed London's elbow as he turned and addressed Michael. "Nothing personal. It's business." And then to London he said, "One of the cars can take you to your next appointment, if you'd like."

"That would be great, Ace. Can you call it for me?"

"It's right around the corner. I'll walk you over there." He extended a hand to Michael. "Mira and our finance office will be in touch with you and your team to get everything squared away."

"For sure, man." They shook hands. "Just make sure I get a ticket to the show." He looked at London. "Front row." Leaned in and kissed her cheek. "Until then, young lady."

London waved as Ace's grip on her elbow tightened slightly. He steered her away. She waited until they'd turned the corner to address him. "That was a fairly possessive move back there, Mr. Montgomery."

"It was meant to be." He eased his hand away from her. They walked in sync, unconsciously, two beautiful people casually strolling on a Thursday night. "No need to say you're welcome. I know you're glad I helped you get away from that presumptuous fool."

"A wealthy fool who's just invested in you."

"He invested in OTB, which was a smart move. I don't have to like a guy to do business with him."

They reached the town car. Ace motioned for the driver to stay seated while he opened the door for London to enter.

Ace got in beside London. "Where's your next appointment?"

"My condo." Ace's face showed his confusion. "I don't really have a meeting. I just didn't want to deal with Michael's ego."

Ace released a chuckle—low and raspy—the kind that sent tingles southbound from London's heart to her heat. "But I didn't do anything for you back there? Okay."

"I could have handled it."

He slid a look her way, one filled with passion, humor and daring.

She leaned over, placed soft cushy lips against his clean-shaven jaw. "Thank you, Ace."

Ace tapped the back of the front seat. "Hey, buddy, take us to my car."

"I thought this car was for me."

"I changed my mind."

He fixed her with a stare from dark brown doe eyes. It was a wrap. Ace got a call from Tyler. London took in the sights and returned a few texts. They reached the garage beneath the office building where OTB was housed. The driver stopped. Ace got out and reached back for London's hand. When she stepped out, he pulled her into a hug.

His lips grazed her ear before he whispered into it. "Thanks for being amazing tonight."

London shuddered, tightened her arms around his waist. Nipples pebbled and feminine muscles clenched. She looked up and didn't know that the desire she saw in his eyes mirrored her own.

"Excuse me a minute. Hey, Randy. Thanks, man." He walked over to the driver's side of the town car and wrapped up business with the driver. London looked around and then walked over to a shiny silver Porsche 911. She ran light fingers over its sleek, smooth design. It reminded her of Ace—exactly the type of car she thought he'd drive.

"You like it?" Ace walked up behind her, placed a hand on her shoulder.

"Very much. It looks brand-new." She turned to him. "Is it?"

Ace shrugged. "It doesn't matter, since that's not the car I'm driving."

"Oh." She scrunched her eyes as she scanned the few remaining cars in the garage for another luxury ride. "Where's your car?"

Ace pointed his key fob toward a ten-plus-year-old SUV. "Right there."

London took in the black GMC with silver accents. Clean. Shiny. A perfectly good car for one of Ace's employees. She never would have guessed it for him. Didn't matter. The way her body hummed with desire for him, he could have rolled up riding a donkey, and in designer duds and five-inch heels she would have jumped straight on that ass.

They got in the car. It smelled manly, musky, like Ace.

"Where are we going?"

"I'm taking you on a tour." He started the engine and eased out of the garage. "You know Ace the model and the famous underwear guy. I want you to see another side."

He reached over and took her hand in his. London felt the same fear she'd experienced all those years ago, that intense feeling that threatened to overwhelm her, to take her to emotional places she'd never been. But this time, the urge London felt wasn't to run away from the feeling. It was to move closer to Ace and make it stronger.

Chapter 10

"We're headed to Oakland?"

"Yep."

"That's where you grew up?"

Ace nodded. "I have some business to handle real quick."

"Not a problem." London looked out the window as they crossed the Bay Bridge. "I don't know why, but I would have guessed you grew up on the East Coast. You have more of that vibe to me."

"I can understand that. Northern California has a bit of that feel. So many easterners moved west and settled here. If you look at San Francisco's architecture and structure, it's a lot like Philly or Boston, definitely nothing like LA."

"That's for sure."

"How'd you like living there? I imagine you fit right in."

"I'm not sure how to take that comment, but yeah, I

loved Los Angeles. Sure, there's a lot of phony people and fake smiles and two-faced ridiculousness, but I didn't have to deal with much of that."

"Maxwell kept you shielded from it?"

"The people in his circle are all successful. They don't have to fake it—they actually live the big life."

"Do you miss it?"

"No. I enjoyed the Hollywood lifestyle, I won't lie about that. His making the movie and me starring in it was the common interest we talked about most and bonded around, really. Outside that, it was always the parties and screenings and dinners, always something going on. But when it was just Max and me—which, with all his assistants and the maid and the chef and the nonstop entertainment schedule, wasn't often—something was missing. I can't explain it other than to say it didn't feel the way forever should. We were in the relationship for very different reasons."

Ace made a disgusted grunt. "I can definitely relate."

"Tell me about it. Since you told me you're all grown-up and only have special sex—" the way she said it made him laugh "—how does that work, exactly?"

"Once you fully commit to a relationship and are then betrayed, it changes you."

They were quiet as Ace exited the bridge onto the I-80. It was late evening. Traffic was still heavy in certain places but he navigated with ease, neo-soul music playing low, caressing London's body the way she wanted Ace to do.

"My mother introduced me to Jessica. They taught at the same school."

"You were engaged to a teacher? Wow, considering the women who've been on your arm, that sounds totally unlike you. She must have been something special."

"She's a beautiful girl. On the outside, anyway. Came across as caring, thoughtful. My mom has a program where she works with young girls, teaches life skills, etiquette and stuff like that. Jessica volunteered to help her, seemed very enthused about shaping young lives. She's a great actor. The girls loved her. She reeled them in, along with my mom…and me."

"What happened?"

"To make a long story short, she wasn't in love with me as much as she was with my money. So much so that she helped herself to quite a lot of it without my knowledge."

"She stole from you?"

"Not in a way I could have had her prosecuted. And believe me, I would have. But yes, she took advantage of the access she had to a couple of my accounts and drained them without asking. I think that was always her agenda. She loved the lifestyle I gave her. I was all in, and she knew it. So there was an underestimation of how I'd react. She tried to excuse her behavior and change the facts, but trust had been broken. It wasn't even about the money. It was about the trust. I forgave her. But I was done.

"It took me a long time to get over that, over a year, really. OTB Her is my woman right now. Totally unpredictable but much more faithful."

They drove by Lake Merritt. It was an area where Ace spent a lot of time as a kid, and he plied her with tales of youthful ignorance. They drove by the school where his mom taught, and the old neighborhood where he'd grown up. London learned the reason Ace had driven over when they stopped by a neighborhood store, one she found out Ace had bought for the man who ran it, a man who'd been like a father figure before his stepfather entered his life. That man was now in the hospital, battling cancer, and the business had suffered because of it. Ace dropped off a loaded debit card to the nineteen-year-old who was running the place in his dad's absence. Told the young man he'd help in any other way he could. That he would do something so selfless didn't go without notice. As they rode back to San Francisco, London was extremely aware that she sat next to a very good man.

Ace headed toward the freeway that would take them back over the bridge. A comfortable silence settled between them as he programmed the address she'd given him into the GPS.

"You're in a condo, not a hotel. Friend of yours?"

"No. It belongs to us."

"Who's us?"

"My family."

"Dang, girl. What does your family do? Y'all own everything!"

"Real estate—I thought I told you."

"When do you think that happened? I just found out your cousins own a vineyard. Wait a minute. The building downtown, Ten Drake Plaza—that's not you, is it?"

"Actually, yes. Owned by the company my dad started in Paradise Cove."

"Is that where you still live?"

"Yes. All of my family is there except a brother who's married and lives in New Orleans, another finishing his doctorate and my sister, Teresa, who splits her time between there and Alaska, where her husband has a business."

"How many of you are there?"

"Eight altogether."

"And you're the baby."

"How'd you guess?"

He gave her a look. "Really?"

"Shut up."

"How long are you going to be in town? Long enough for us to get a fitting in tomorrow?"

"Sure."

"Any plans for tonight?"

"Yes, with you."

"There you go again. Acting like London, when a strong brother like me needs to hang with Clarisse."

"Ace, I'd like very much for you to come in and share a cup of tea and then tuck me into bed."

"That's all you want from me in bed...a little tucking?"

"I want a lot of tucking from you, Ace. But this is all about business, right?"

"Right," Ace said with a serious face London thought worthy of an Oscar. If Ace came inside the condo tonight, she'd make sure he didn't leave until morning.

Chapter 11

They arrived back in San Francisco. GPS directed Ace to an upscale neighborhood on the city's upper south side.

"In a quarter of a mile, your destination is on the right."

Ace glanced at London. "This is where your condo is, Presidio Heights?"

"Not mine. My family owns it."

"You almost could have walked from the restaurant."

"In these heels? I don't think so."

"You know I'm kidding. I wouldn't have let you walk home, heels or not."

"Ah, you're such a gentleman."

"I try."

"I'm going to try, too."

"What?"

"Never mind. Take a left at the next stop and then your first right to the garage."

The two kept up a casual banter until they reached the living room.

Ace stopped in the middle of the floor, hands on hips as he looked around. "This is very nice. Was it professionally decorated?"

"My mom would love hearing that question. She's furnished so many houses that calling her a professional is probably not too much of a stretch."

"It sounds like you have a wonderful family."

"They're all right. Let me take your coat." He peeled out of it. She hung both of theirs in the hall closet and continued to the kitchen. "What type of tea would you like?"

He followed her. "What type do you have?"

She turned and stopped him. "Why don't I make you a special caramel and cinnamon blend while you light the fireplace and find some good music on the sound system?"

"That'll work." He returned to the living room. "Where is it?"

"The fireplace? It's that big open square on the far wall."

"Stick to your job as a model," he yelled, "because you suck as a comedian!"

"You know you laughed. The stereo is controlled by that panel near the hallway. Push the button to the right to open it up and turn it on. Everything is self-explanatory from there."

London poured water into the teakettle, pulled down a box of assorted teas and then went to the pantry for one of two types of caramel she intended to serve with the tea. Soon, the neo-soul sounds of Amel Larrieux floated around the wall and into the kitchen.

"Great choice."

She heard fingers popping, smiled when she saw the lights dim. The teapot hissed, mimicking the heat London felt between her legs. She dressed the tea just the way she liked it and hoped Ace would, too. After unwrapping the other caramel ingredient, she picked up the mugs and edged toward the living room to peep Ace's location. He sat on the couch, head bobbing. She imagined his eyes closed. Perfect. Her stilettos made soft clicks against the hardwood floor as she walked into the room.

He slowly lifted and turned his head, then jerked his whole body around. "London!"

"What?" She continued toward him, completely naked except for the heels.

"What is this?"

She placed the mugs on the table and climbed on Ace's lap. He was too shocked to move. It was exactly as she'd expected and hoped. She then reached around for one of the mugs. "It's cinnamon tea with a caramel twist."

"The caramel being you?"

"Some of it. Here. Taste."

"London…"

"Shh. Just taste it."

He blew on the hot concoction, then took a sip. "It's delicious."

She set down the cup. "Now, taste this."

Her head lowered. She placed determined lips over his, swallowed his objection and felt a part of Ace's anatomy coming out of shock. A slow grinding of her hips encouraged this unruly member to keep doing what came naturally.

"London, stop…" An objection, true enough, but without much conviction.

She outlined his lips with her tongue, slid it to the earlobe she remembered as sensitive and swirled it inside.

"You know we can't do this," he whispered, even as his hands slowly, almost begrudgingly, came up and cupped her booty.

"We can, and we should," she whispered. Running her hands across his chest, she bypassed the buttons on his shirt and went straight for the belt buckle. Who knew how long the shock would last? She reached back for the packet she'd set next to her mug. "I promise to give you Clarisse Alana tomorrow," she said, ripping open the packaging with her teeth and retrieving its contents. "Let me be London tonight."

He'd been stiff, guarded, but either at her request or the sound of foil being torn, his body relaxed. Strong thighs that could have made him a star of track and field as well as the runway lifted them both up slightly, enough for him to slide the slacks down and expose a pair of the underwear he'd made famous.

London didn't hesitate. Her body already thrumming, her folds already slick with anticipation, she reached between her legs, slipped the condom around his missile, and guided it home. With a sigh, Ace leaned toward the nipple within sight and gently pulled it into his mouth. He placed his hands around London's taut waist and aided her exuberant ride. Up. Down. Swirl. Grind. The connection was electric. Their sexes were a perfect fit. Both had been without it for too long. When London's pants increased and soft oohs spilled from her mouth, Ace put those thigh muscles to work, repeatedly tapped her hot spot and sent them both over the edge.

Ace had barely stopped pulsating before lifting London off his lap and into his arms. He stood. "Where's the bedroom?"

"Upstairs. But that's okay. I'll wash off in a bit."

"Wash off? Do you think this is over? You started this, London, against my wishes. Now I'm going to finish it."

Several positions and a few hours later, Ace had done just that.

The next morning found the two lovebirds totally satiated, sexually satisfied and absolutely starved. London went downstairs and pulled a menu from one of several kept in a kitchen drawer. An hour later the table was laden with enough food to feed a family: blueberry waffles, turkey bacon, pork sausage, scrambled eggs, English muffins, hash browns and, for Ace, a pot of coffee, piping hot.

"Food's here!"

Ace ambled down the stairs, his hair still damp, body fresh from the shower. At London's suggestion he'd scrounged through drawers and closets and found a black button-up and a pair of black jeans. He looked like what he was: model, lover, boss, conducting business on his cell phone as he entered the room. London had put her freshly washed hair up into a ponytail and pulled on a halter-style minidress. She had no idea whether it belonged to her sister, Teresa, or one of her brothers' exlovers. Whoever it was she thanked them. It was cute, loose and comfortable, and since she wore no underwear, it would provide quick and easy access to what she hoped for—another lovemaking round.

"Shoot the pictures over and I'll have a look," Ace said, his brows arched and eyes wide at the amount of food. "She's still in town, so I'll see if we can get her in for a fitting. No, don't worry about it. I was going to call her anyway." He kissed London's lips softly and gave her a wink. "This afternoon, say around one?" He reached for a cup and poured coffee into it. "Let's arrange a tentative photo shoot, as well. Lucien is sending over pics of some of the finished pieces. We can take the publicist's advice and use them to start creating buzz for the show." He nodded and sipped, picked up a link of sausage and took a bite. "Listen, Mira, I need to run. We'll meet later at the office. I should be there around ten or so. All right, let's talk then."

He hung up, pulled London into an embrace and then set her away from him for a head-to-toe scan. "I thought you said I'd see Clarisse this morning."

"You are seeing her," London said, pairing a demure look with the innocent-sounding delivery.

"All that leg I'm looking at screams London. Clarisse would have on a maxidress."

"Guess I'm rubbing off on her a bit. Dig in! I know you're hungry, because I'm starved."

"Yeah, and you worked me like a sex slave."

"You seemed to enjoy it."

"Think we've got enough food?"

London laughed. "This is what happens when you order while hungry. Their food is good, though." They loaded up their plates and sat down. "Bon appétit."

For several seconds the only conversation was between the silverware, the china and the food. After putting away a good chunk of the meal, Ace wiped his mouth with a napkin and reached for the coffeepot. "Whatever happened with those flowers you asked me about, the ones you thought came from me. Did you find out who sent them?"

"No. Diamond, my cousin, looked into it for me. But the floral company's privacy policy forbade them from giving her the name of who purchased them."

"What did the card say?"

"There wasn't one. You'd think someone who'd send an extravagant gift like that would want credit. That's why I assumed it was you. Because there wasn't a card and we'd spent the previous day together."

"It's an upscale hotel with affluent clients. It could have been anyone who saw you there."

"I guess."

"Speaking of seeing you, is there any way you can come to our offices for a fitting today? Lucien has a few pieces ready, and as much as I enjoy you without clothes, I can't wait to see you in them."

"I'm staying until Sunday, so sure, I can come by."

"Oh, really? Plans in the big city, huh?"

"My sister-in-law's best friend lives here part-time and is in town now. Oh, it's Trent. For a sec I forgot you know him. Anyway, Quinn is flying up tonight and we're going to hang out a couple days and go home on Saturday.

"What are you doing tonight? We don't have any firm plans yet, but maybe you can join us."

"I don't know. We'll see."

Casual chitchat continued as both refilled and demolished a second plate. Ace's email and text indicators pinged throughout. After receiving an urgent one from Mira regarding a world-renowned photographer lined up for the shoot, he finished the glass of water London had poured him and stood.

"Thank you for an unexpected yet amazing evening, and a delicious breakfast. Duty calls. I've got to go."

She stood, as well. Together they climbed the steps to the master suite and found Ace's clothes, the evidence of hasty disrobing evident in pants inside out and a shirt thrown across the room.

"You can wear the jeans if you want and either keep them or give them to me later."

He nodded and gathered his things.

"Let me find a tote for you."

She did, and after placing his clothes inside the black leather bag, they headed back downstairs to the garage.

They reached the door leading out. Ace turned to face her. "You know we can't do this again, right?"

"I know of no such thing."

"Well, we can't. Doing business together is complicated enough without adding sexual tension, romantic assumptions and possible misunderstandings."

"The only sexual tension that will happen is if you try and keep that delicious dick away from me." She opened the door. "I don't want to argue, and you've got to go." She gave him a quick kiss while gently pushing him out the door. "You said one, right?" Ace nodded. "I won't be late."

He reached his car door and opened it. "I'm going to make sure of that. A car will be by for you at twelve thirty."

London closed the door and leaned against it. Not do it again? Was he crazy? Over the next few weeks they'd be working together closely. London planned not only to do it again, but as often as possible.

Chapter 12

"I like everything you've made. All of this! It's not easy to impress in this business, but... Wow."

Ace, London, Lucien and Tyler stood in the middle of a cluttered warehouse showroom. Clothes in various stages of completion hung on mannequins and hangers, and lay draped across furniture. At Ace's request, Lucien had brought out four of the almost forty looks that would be presented during the four-week period when major label shows were held.

London could feel Ace's eyes following her as she eyed each piece and ran a casual hand over the material or design accent. She said nothing but loved everything designed for the fall collection, including a cropped faux fur–trimmed sweater and cigarette pant look, an over-size hoodie-inspired top paired with leggings and thigh-high boots, and a wide-legged jumpsuit accented with the same cranberry-colored faux fur as the sweater. All were done in tan silks, suedes and cashmere. But it was the show's trench-inspired closeout piece that dropped London's jaw. The sketch she'd seen earlier didn't compare to the finished design. The coat-dress material was a shiny silk charmeuse, the exact color of London's skin. She looked from the dress Lucien held to the design beside it, noted the wide alligator belt, cranberry fur accents and exaggerated skirt.

"Now I understand the stilts."

"We've got a guy working on them, and they're actually kind of nice," Ace replied. "Almost like shoes. Might start a trend. Let's get you in some of this, see if we can make the magic happen."

Ace was nervous. He told himself it was ridiculous, that he'd done dozens of fittings and had himself been fitted thousands of times. That he'd seen more naked women than most small-town doctors. That if you'd seen one naked model, you'd seen them all. He told himself all that. And knew it was BS. After last night with London and their heated, prolonged, seductive goodbye, he knew he'd be lucky to hear her voice let alone see her face without his flagpole rising.

Turned out the nervousness was warranted. When London shrugged out of her coat, peeled off her top and exposed the nipples he'd suckled half the night and part of the morning, Ace was not prepared. She shimmied out of her pants. Cotton panties had never looked sexier. His heart thudded. His groin clutched. He wanted to wrap her in his jacket and shield her breasts from a workroom filled with some of the gayest guys in San Francisco. Ace could have kicked himself. He knew how strong his feelings had been before. They seemed to have gotten worse. Getting physical with London? *Bad choice, brother. Very bad choice.*

But her body in his clothes? Perfect.

Lucien agreed. "You look delicious! Your body is better than a mannequin. Look—" he stepped forward and clutched the material at her waist "—I need to take it up here." He turned her around, adjusted the material covering her butt. "And maybe take out a little from each seam. A big derriere, tiny waist and so beautiful! Just looking at you and I almost turn straight!"

"All right, enough flirting, Lucien. But he's right. I really liked this on the hanger. But on you, it definitely goes to another level." He looked around for one of a half dozen assistants helping Lucien with the collection. "Hey, can one of you guys bring a crate over? Let's get her in the trench," Ace said to Lucien as he turned back around. A young man brought over a crate. Ace helped London into the dress. Wanting to try a range of accessories Lucien bypassed the alligator belt on the sketch and brought back a wide gold belt from the accessory wall. He cinched it tightly, make London's waist appear even more concave. Ace propped up the exaggerated collar, adjusted the fabric so that the V opening reached her navel.

"Glitter," he mumbled.

Lucien stepped closer. "The gold works better, huh?"

Ace nodded. "I thought the leather was it for sure, but seeing it on her, you're right. With her body shimmering with glitter. That, the dress, nothing more." Who needed jewelry when one shined as bright as his muse?

He tapped his phone and put the call on speaker. "Dent, is hair and makeup here?"

"Yes. Where should they set up? Where are we shooting?"

Ace eyed London thoughtfully, looked around the

warehouse and then out the window at the overcast sky. "Bring them to one of the spare rooms over here. We're shooting on the roof."

Once set up, London went for hair and makeup. Ace returned to his office, closed the door, had his calls held and paced. He knew making love to her was wrong. Now he questioned the wisdom of choosing her as the face of OTB Her. Being anywhere around her turned him on. He didn't even have to see her, just know she was in the room. Everything about her was amazing, even the parts of her personality that got on his nerves. This woman had been kryptonite years ago. She was even more beautiful now. What in the heck was he thinking?

Ace hadn't a clue, but in times like these he knew he could reach out to his best friend for an intelligent answer. He pulled out his cell phone and sat at his desk. It was the middle of a workday, but sometimes life had to be interrupted.

The call was answered on the second ring.

Ace exhaled. "Hey, Mom."

"Hello, son. How are you? Is everything okay?"

"Everything's fine." *Not.* "I know you're still in the middle of your school day and won't hold you long."

"Your timing is perfect, actually. My kids are in study hall. I was on my way to the teachers' lounge but will slip outside instead." He heard Christine speak to someone and could tell from the shift in background noise that she was now outside. "Whew, I didn't know it was so chilly out. Feels good, though. The day's been dragging. This will wake me up."

Crap! He hadn't even considered the weather. Was it too cold for them to shoot outside? And on the roof, no less, where it would be even colder? Granted, it was the showing of their fall collection, so the clothes would provide some warmth. Models often braved much worse—fur coats in summer, bikinis in snow. London was a professional and was sure to pull off whatever look the photographer required. Were it anyone else it wouldn't have mattered. He wouldn't have given the model's comfort a second thought. But this wasn't just another model. It was London. Clarisse Alana. His muse.

"Sorry for rambling. Even though you said you're fine, I know you didn't call to chat about the weather."

"Remember that makeup commercial you loved, the one where the model came up out of the water? You went and bought some of it even though I've never seen you wear makeup much. Remember?"

"Of course, I remember that pretty girl. When you told me you knew her, I suggested y'all get married. Do you remember that?"

Ace laughed. "I was hoping you'd forgotten that part." At that time she'd also said Ace and London would make pretty babies. Hopefully she'd forgotten that, too. Even though doing what it took to make babies with London was the best time he'd ever had.

"I ran into her last weekend."

"Oh, really? In San Francisco?"

"No, I took a little break, went out of town."

"You? A break? You stopped working and didn't tell me?"

"It was a last-minute decision, one I didn't make. I was being a bear in the office. The partners threatened to oust me if I didn't go get some rest. Anyway, Frida booked me at a resort in Southern California. London was there."

"Really? Tell me more!"

"Turns out her family owns the property. Crazy co-incidence, huh?"

"You know I say coincidence is just God being anonymous. Is she still modeling?"

"Absolutely."

"I read where she broke up with that rich director. He's cute enough, but I never thought he was the right one for her."

"You read the tabloids?"

"No, but I watch those entertainment shows sometimes. Guilty pleasure. I think I saw the news on *XYZ*. Sounds like both of you are single. Are you two dating?"

"No, but I asked her to be the face of my new line."

"Oh, son, that's great news. I love it! She'll be perfect."

"That's what I thought, too. But now I realize there may be a problem."

"What?"

"I used to have feelings for her years ago. There's still an attraction."

"And that's a problem because?"

"Because it complicates the workplace. I don't need the drama. Don't know if I can handle the distraction. It might be too much."

"Sounds like a challenge. My son doesn't usually run from those. Will she be at the show in New York?"

Ace sighed. "I guess."

"I'd like to meet her."

"Mom, I'm calling to discuss what I perceive as a problem and your answer is that you want to meet my problem. What's wrong with this picture?"

"There's nothing wrong with the picture, son. Everything about the picture might be right. And that's what scares you. Don't let what happened with Jessica rob you of a life with the right woman. I can tell you from personal experience that there's nothing like living life with the one you love."

"How is Hank?"

"Your stepfather is fine. He's not coming to the show, though. Says he doesn't do froufrou stuff."

"But you still want two tickets, right?"

"I'll let you know."

The office phone rang.

"Hold on a moment, Mom." He muted the cell phone and picked up the landline's receiver. "This is Ace."

"Ace, it's Tyler. The photographer's here and everything's set. We're ready for your direction."

"On my way." He switched calls and headed toward the door. "Mom, I've got to go take care of business."

"All I have to say is that hopefully part of that business includes London."

He ended the call and headed to the warehouse where Tyler and Lucien were coordinating looks. Ace was ready to decide on outfits but braced himself to endure London's photo shoot. No doubt she would look incredibly stunning, beyond desirable, good enough to eat. And Ace knew from last night's experience she was one tasty treat.

Definitely a problem, but maybe his mom was right. London Drake just might turn out to be the best darn problem he'd ever had.

Chapter 13

It did not surprise Ace that London was good. She'd been modeling for years, had done hundreds of shoots and was the utmost professional. Yet he hadn't expected her to be all that she was that night. The shoot took hours. Her hair was filled with waist-length extensions. Headache heavy, Ace assumed. The stilts were high, hard, uncomfortable and necessary for most of the shots. There was not one complaint. She didn't just wear the clothes. She embodied them, made them come alive. As the photographer and crew set up the last shot of the night, Mira joined Tyler and Ace on the roof. It began to rain.

Ace frowned at the sky. "You couldn't wait another ten minutes?"

"It looks like that's a wrap," Mira said. "See you two inside."

"I was hoping, too, bro." Tyler took an umbrella from an astute assistant and passed one to Ace.

The two watched a flurry of activity on the other side of the roof. Assistants rushed to London, one with a tarp, another with an umbrella, a third with a stepladder to help her down. London called the photographer over.

"I'm going to go see if she can come in tomorrow and finish the shoot," Ace said to Tyler, already walking toward the group.

Tyler nodded and turned to go inside. London was still on the ledge, huddled under the tarp. The photographer was bent over his equipment case. Ace decided to start there. No need to see if London was available if the photographer was already booked.

"What do you think? Did we get enough for some great ads or should I add another day?"

"Yes and no," the photographer said, rising, another camera in hand. "Is that material waterproof?"

"What? Her dress?"

"Yes. London wants to shoot in the rain. Will it ruin the garment?"

Ace's brow creased. Models took orders. They didn't give them. As for the material, Ace hadn't a clue how it would respond. He looked over to see if Lucien was among the people surrounding her. What he saw made him forget about everything but getting the shot.

The belt had been removed. The coat was pulled off her shoulders, almost to her waist, loads of fabric pooled at her feet. Strategically placed tendrils of her hair helped maintain modesty while offering up a fantasy for anyone who saw the pic. She crouched on the ledge, her limbs positioned in that broken-doll style that couture models mastered, her head tilting back to welcome the rain. Ace thought of his mom and their recent conversation about the shot Christine had loved, the one where London rose out of the water, her face perfectly made up. She looked that way now, only better, like a nymph, a siren, some otherworldly creature come to beguile, snatch and tame men's hearts.

The photographer swirled around her like a dancer, turning his waterproof camera from one angle to the next. Hovering over her. Lying beside her. Crouching beneath her to get the best shots. And like the perfect partner, London innately matched her pose to his flow, inspired him with her boldness, propelled his artistry with her own. A clap of thunder sounded. Lightning backlit the moment, allowed the quick-thinking photographer to exchange his flashes with those nature provided. He looked at the shot and yelled with excitement.

"I just took the shot of my lifetime. Ace, it's a wrap!"

Ace watched the photographer run over to London. He showed her the picture. They kissed and hugged in creative bliss. A wave of jealousy and possessiveness came over Ace, slammed into him harder than the raindrops now falling. The fog of denial lifted. The truth became clear. London was more than a friend, more than a muse. She was his soul mate. Theirs was more than an attraction or sexual chemistry. They fit together so well because their union was meant to be. Ace was surer of this than he'd ever been of anything in his life. Now he needed to convince London.

Fifteen minutes later, Ace walked into London's makeshift dressing room. She'd shed the wet clothes and sat wrapped in a large terry-cloth robe, sipping hot tea, while a stylist blow-dried the thick extensions. Ace had changed, too. The black button-down, black jeans, black leather boots and dark expression made him look as dangerous as the storm outside.

"Amazing work out there today, London." He reached her, leaned down and kissed her forehead.

"You think so?" He nodded. "Then you should let your face know." And then to the stylist, she said, "I'll finish it. Thanks."

Ace moved a stack of clothes from the chair across from her and sat down. "What do you mean?"

London studied him as she piled the damp tendrils atop her head, wound them into a topknot and secured it with a wide band. "You walked in looking like a thunder-cloud."

"Sorry about that. Got a lot on my mind. Those rain shots changed the entire layout of our campaign. Mira's on the phone now, calling in the entire PR team. You're worth it. This line has gone to a whole other level, and it's because of who you are."

"Sounds like you might prefer London to Clarisse after all?"

"I'm beginning to see that both sides have their ben-efits. London earned her high paycheck today. We'll be up all night, but that's all right. I'm too excited to sleep anyway."

"Oh, Ace. Not all night! I wanted you to go out with me and my friends."

"Sorry, babe. Work before pleasure." His ringtone sounded. He looked at the phone's face and stood. "Speaking of which, this is Mira now. I'll call you later." He walked over and kissed her again. But it was differ-ent this time. They were alone, so he allowed himself a moment to savor the lips that had glistened in the down-pour. To use his tongue and outline their fullness before swiping the crease and demanding entry inside. Then another moment to swirl his tongue with hers, to let his hand drop behind the cloth and tweak the nipple already hardening at his touch. One moment more to sear her body with memories of what they'd shared before and promises of more to come.

"You drive me crazy," he whispered as he pulled away.

London laughed as she stood, shed the robe and unveiled her nakedness. "Will you return the favor?"

"Girl!" Ace backed away. "Nothing but trouble. Just like I said. Let me get out of here while I still can."

As the limo pulled up to the condo, London noticed lights inside. She hurriedly thanked the driver, barely giving him time to open the door before she was out of the car and through the unlocked door.

"Quinn!"

"We're in here!"

London walked down a short hall to a sitting room. Quinn Taylor-Drake looked around and screeched. "Oh, my goodness... Your hair!"

Trent Corrigan, who'd been sitting next to Quinn, jumped up and ran over. "All right, girl," he purred as London swung the now-dry hair she'd let down in the car. "You'd better work those ten packs of hair, girl."

"Ha! More like twenty."

"I love it, London." Quinn came over, too, and fingered the long locks. "They did this for the shoot?"

"Yes, and after sitting in that chair for almost two hours, I am determined to wear them for more than a day."

"You look totally different," Quinn said.

"She looks totally hot," Trent added. "Where are we going to shake it up tonight? I'm ready to par-tay!"

The three went to dinner at a restaurant run by one of Trent's friends. It was in the Castro, one of the first openly gay neighborhoods in the United States. Located near the highly trafficked intersection of Castro and Market Streets, Pride & Good Prices was as much a place to socialize and meet up as it was a spot where one could get gourmet-quality international cuisine at reasonable prices. Reservations were highly encouraged, but you could always get seated when you were friends with the owner.

After a complimentary glass of wine during their ten-minute wait for a table, during which notice of London produced selfies galore, the three were seated in a corner booth.

"We don't need menus," Trent told the cute bald waiter who had skin smoother than London's and whose makeup was on point. "Just tell the chef to serve up some good food." And then he turned to London. "I can't get over you and all that hair, honey. I think the last time we partied, you were wearing a Halle Berry cut."

"If you saw my hair that short, it was a wig. Either way, it was a long time ago."

"She tried to act like she didn't remember you," Quinn said. "But when I mentioned Cannes, fireworks, chalet and champagne in the same sentence, the memories flooded back."

Quinn and London were the same age and had both spent their high school years in Swiss boarding schools, but Trent was how they'd eventually met. He'd dabbled in modeling and through a connection had been offered a chalet during the film festival in Cannes. He'd invited Quinn, his best friend, to come, too. When he saw London, whom he'd done a show with just weeks prior, he'd invited her to a party at the chalet. The luxury villa was seated on a hilltop, with stunning views of the sea and city. Dom Pérignon had flowed like water. At midnight, a loud, gargantuan fireworks display had shocked and delighted the revelers from their unobstructed view.

"Remember what you said, Trent?" Quinn asked, once Trent had recalled his version of the story. "'The trumpets have sounded. The heavens have opened. Let the skinny-dipping begin!'"

"I almost recreated that scene earlier tonight," London said, laughing.

Quinn's eyes widened. "You posed nude?"

"Not quite." London told them about shooting in the rain and being inspired to make the most of it.

They made quick work of all-American entrées and continued to chat. Trent hailed a taxi for the next place he'd planned for them, a private club with a sign at the entrance: Only Wild Child Allowed.

And wild it was. As London's eyes adjusted to the dim lighting, her thoughts went to one of the co-owners of Incomparable, her modeling agency, a former model who'd spent her teen years at the New York disco Studio 54. What London saw now was how she'd imagined the antics shared about the popular seventies' disco. Outlandish costumes. Artistic expression. Various phases of nudity. Everyone happy and having a good time.

So much so that when the excited young blond wearing a cowboy hat, leather chaps, alligator boots and jeans that exposed his butt cheeks pulled her over to dance between him and his partner, who wore tuxedo pants, a polka-dot bow tie and a smile, London thought nothing about it. Because of the strobing disco lights, she didn't see the flash.

Before dawn the next morning, London would once again make headlines. But Ace and the rest of the world would know about it before she had a clue.

Chapter 14

His alarm went off at 9:00 a.m. Eyes still shut, Ace fumbled around for the knob and shut it off. Five minutes later, his text indicator buzzed. He ignored it, too. Didn't bother to answer the cell phone when it rang ten minutes after that, but when his landline chimed only seconds later, he jerked up the receiver.

"What!"

A brief pause and then, "So you've seen them."

Rubbing his eyes, Ace propped himself up against the headboard. "Dent? What the hell? We spent half the night looking at those pictures and the rest making sure they got out to all the right sources."

"No, not the ones from the shoot. The ones of London stirring up valuable publicity to make our upcoming press releases even more newsworthy. Even though she wasn't wearing our clothes."

"Oh, man." Ace placed the call on speaker and snatched a small tablet off his nightstand. "Was she wearing any?"

Tyler chuckled. "A butt was exposed, but it wasn't hers."

Ace typed London's name into the search engine. Half a dozen news links came up along with a picture. London, laughing, sandwiched between two guys. One dancing provocatively behind her, cheek to cheek, one might say, while the other held her in what appeared to be a sizzling kiss.

The thought of her in another man's arms was enough to skyrocket his blood pressure. Seeing it made Ace think of kicking ass and taking names, and he wasn't a violent man. It also pushed away the deep sleep that moments ago was the only thing he wanted. Now he wanted to find London and whoever this guy was and strangle him. Or her. Or both.

He tapped on the notorious website, *XYZ*, which had broken the story. Toward the end of the first paragraph, he began to read out loud.

"'London, who recently ended a relationship with megarich director Maxwell Tata, creator of the wildly successful fanatica—fantasy combined with erotica—films, seems to have moved on from her lover…but in what direction? One moment she was seen giggling and hugging a pretty young woman as they exited the bathroom. The next one had her lip-locked with a gay—or maybe bi?—man in the middle of the dance floor. No details on who she went home with, but whoever the lucky choice was, looks like they had fun.'"

Ace tossed the tablet on the bed, threw back the sheets and hopped out of bed. The article's last line was like a bucket of water on his face, chasing any chance or desire of sleep away faster than a double espresso.

"We probably should have said something during that first meeting, but she's representing OTB now and needs to watch her ways," he told Tyler, after snatching up the cordless receiver and beginning to pace.

"Are you kidding me? This is fabulous press."

"This is a scandal and drama that I don't need."

"Have you forgotten our company's name?"

The company and Ace's last statement had nothing to do with each other. But he eyed his naked frame as he crossed a mirror in his pacing and kept that truth to himself.

"OTB stands for 'Out of the Box.' That's exactly the message these articles portray. With the money shots we took last night, our new tagline and London's celebrity? We'll probably get moved to a bigger space in New York and will definitely get a prime-time spot."

When they'd coined the line around 2:00 a.m., Ace thought the tagline Reigning Over Her was genius. But if pictures like these began dominating celebrity websites, the statement would take on a whole other meaning.

"Have you talked to the PR team?"

"No," Tyler responded. "They're my next call."

"I suggest we stay away from this tagline. Maybe push back those ads a day or two. Once Mira hears about this I'm sure she'll agree."

"Negative, Ace. Mira called me, beyond excited. You're going to get outvoted on this one."

Damn.

"I'll be in the office in a couple hours. Don't do anything until I get there."

Ace placed the receiver back in the cradle and reached for his cell phone. He was calmer now but still ticked at London. There was a lot on the line with this new unveiling, chiefly Ace's name and reputation in the fashion industry. London needed to understand that as long as she was the face for OTB Her, their lives were intertwined. Mud thrown on her got him dirty. He wanted to stay clean, and planned to.

"Ace?" Her voice was scratchy and groggy sounding, evidence she'd just woken up.

"I'd say I'm sorry, except you're why I'm awake."

"Huh?"

"No one has told you yet?"

"Told me what?"

"That you're trending right now, and all over the news."

"You woke me up to tell me that?" Ace heard a sound and could imagine her frowning and flopping back down on the bed. "I thought there was an emergency or something, like my house was on fire or someone died."

"Someone's about to. Who's the dude you were kissing?"

"Excuse me?" she replied, all grogginess gone.

"You heard me. There's a picture with you and two guys dancing, one rubbing your butt and the other all in your face."

"Hold on."

Ace slipped on a pair of shorts and padded downstairs in bare feet.

"This picture posted by *XYZ*?"

He reached the kitchen and fired up his Keurig machine. "They're one of several sources reporting the story."

"There's a story, too? And you believed whatever it said?"

"I was doubtful about you and the woman, but describing that picture doesn't take a thousand words."

"No, it only takes a few truthful ones. Look, you've been in this industry longer than me and should know how the game is played. If we're going to work together, you're going to have to learn where to put your trust, and it's not in a tabloid or entertainment website."

"Wait, you can't talk to me like that. I called to bawl you out."

"You might want to make sure you have your facts straight first."

"Are you going to tell me you weren't kissing that guy?"

"That's exactly what I'm going to say."

"Really, London? You're going to lie to my face like that?"

"I'm telling the truth. Look at the angle of the picture. Do you actually see our faces? No. The paparazzi framed the picture to make it look like we're kissing. I remember this moment. I'd asked him the regime to his buffed-out body. He made a joke. I couldn't hear him over the loud music. So he pulled me to him. His mouth is closer to my ear than my lips. But since you obviously think I'm a promiscuous tramp, you drew your own conclusions."

"I don't think that about you."

"Yet you call at an ungodly hour and wake me up to argue about a tabloid story."

Put that way, Ace's anger began to deflate. A little embarrassment replaced it. But only a little.

"Who's the woman mentioned in the story?"

"Quinn, my sister-in-law, Detective," London sarcastically replied. "Any more questions?"

"Only a couple before I wrap up this investigation," he said in all seriousness. "Where were you?"

"The Castro, one of Trent's many playgrounds. We were at a private club, so I may have let down my guard and been a little freer than I would have at a public venue. Though when I think about it, paparazzi being there makes total sense. I saw a couple actors there—one an

A-list heartthrob who is living life on the down low. At one point I saw him pushed up on his secret boyfriend. The photog obviously missed that action. And that would have been the money shot, a story way worthier than me out with my sister-in-law and her best friend."

"I apologize for jumping to conclusions and waking you up. But can I ask a favor?"

"Sure."

"Try and remember that you're representing something that is very important to me, something near and dear to my heart. After this weekend, anything you do will get tied to OTB Her. So can you please keep any scandals toned down and to a minimum?"

"Only if you'll promise me something, too."

Suspicion was evident in Ace's hesitation. But he asked anyway. "What?"

"Come over later so we can do some scandalous things...together?"

"I'd love nothing better, but there's no way I can get away today."

"What about tonight, or tomorrow?"

"I thought you were leaving tomorrow."

"Given the right incentive, I could stay another day. I need to talk over something with you anyway."

"I've got about eight or nine incentives. Are you interested?"

"The way those incentives feel inside me, stroke after delicious stroke? Consider my plans changed!"

They laughed as Ace ended the call. He told himself he'd handled the situation, but he went through the day unable to shake the feeling that he'd gotten got instead.

Chapter 15

London walked into the bedroom where Quinn had slept Friday night. "I didn't even think to ask what flight you'd booked us on. Why are you leaving so early?"

"Because of a controlling man named Ike. You may have heard of him?"

"Vaguely, but I try to keep my distance," London teased. "We don't see eye to eye."

"Considering yesterday's headlines, you may want to keep it that way."

The women laughed. A year ago, Quinn had married London's oldest brother, Ike Jr., ten years older than both London and Quinn. London was barely eight years old when Ike went off to college, and she'd moved to a Swiss boarding school by the time he returned. The age gap, distance and difference in moral viewpoints often kept the stubborn siblings in bicker mode. It had initially been that way with him and Quinn. Like London, she was free-spirited and spontaneous. She was proof that opposites could indeed attract, but Quinn had learned it also made certain areas of life tricky to navigate. Ike's treating her like the center of his universe made these ministrations not only bearable but worth every frustrating minute.

"Are you sure you can't stay and go home with me tomorrow?"

Quinn looked over at London as she continued to pack her bag. "As if you want me to. I know you said there was nothing going on between you two, but the look in your eyes every time you mention Ace's name begs to differ."

"I said we weren't dating. That doesn't mean we're not having sex."

"London!" Quinn stopped packing and plopped cross-legged on the bed. "You said after Max you were taking a break. Wanted to get your head clear, focus on you."

London fell back with an exaggerated sigh. "I couldn't help myself."

"Has Max stopped calling?"

"Not completely, but he doesn't blow my phone up the way he used to. Or make every conversation about us getting back together. Now when we talk, it's just a friend thing."

"I thought Max was a pretty good catch."

"At one time, so did I."

"Are you sure Papa Dee didn't have an indirect hand in this rekindled romance?"

"Maybe. Nothing happened in Temecula, much to my chagrin. But I kept at it, and my first night here in the condo I finally wore him down."

"Ooh, you are so bad."

"Troublemaker is what he calls me."

"Well, it's obvious he makes you happy. I never saw

Maxwell put that type of smile on your face. So what do you two have planned for the rest of the day?"

"I don't know about him, but I plan to get into as much…trouble…as I possibly can."

Quinn had only been gone thirty minutes or so when Ace rang London's phone.

"Hey, you! Can't find parking? Just come around the back and I'll open the garage."

"What did I say earlier on the phone? That I'd be by to pick you up."

"I know, but you've been so busy and I spent the last two days out with friends. I thought we could just, you know, enjoy a quiet afternoon watching movies and stuff."

"Watching movies, huh? That's hardly what's on your mind, you nympho. Put some clothes on, because you're probably butt naked."

"No, I'm not!" London said amid laughter, because booty shorts, a tank top and no bra hardly qualified as fully dressed.

"And you're right. Parking is lousy, so I'm in the middle of the street. Put on something casual with comfortable shoes. And don't keep me waiting."

"Just come in for a—hello? Hello?" London let out an exasperated huff and stomped up the stairs. But her heart was smiling.

She exchanged the booty shorts for brushed corduroy leggings, pulled on a bulky sweater over the tank and grabbed the most comfortable shoes in the closet, a pair of boots with a three-inch wedge heel. She pulled her Rapunzel-like extensions into a loose braid and secured it at the bottom with a hair band. After grabbing her purse, keys and shades off the bar counter that separated the kitchen from a breakfast nook, she set the house alarm and walked out the door. Ace was double-parked in front of her house leaning against a gleaming silver Porsche, the one she'd seen the other night in his company's garage. He was on the phone but ended the call as she approached, and opened her door.

"I thought you said this wasn't your car." She gave him a playful pop upside the head as she slid into the buttery leather seat.

He closed the door and leaned into the car through the open window. "Woman, you're going to have to learn to keep your hands off me." He gave her a quick peck before going around the front of the car, waving an apology at the car honking behind them, and got inside.

He shifted the car into gear and took off.

"Did you borrow your partner's car? You didn't have to do that."

"Wow. Thank you, Clarisse."

"I didn't mind riding in your old jalopy."

Ace burst out laughing. "Sorry, my bad. It's definitely London in the car." He turned on the radio and smoothly navigated the city's crowded streets toward the interstate. "I didn't tell you this wasn't my car. I told you it wasn't the car we were riding in that night. The SUV— or, excuse me, my jalopy—is a safer bet in some parts of Oakland."

"I was just teasing, Ace. Your other car is perfectly fine."

"I know it is. But when given the choice, I prefer driving this one."

"And I prefer riding in it. This is nice!"

"Thank you."

"Why didn't you want to come inside just now?"

"Because I knew if I did we'd be in bed within ten

minutes. We've spent more time having sex than talking. I didn't want to spend the day that way."

"Jeez. I don't know whether I should be flattered or offended."

"Flattered, definitely." He beat out a little of the rhythm from a nineties' throwback that played in the background. "Even though we've known each other for years, I don't know that much about you. Heck, until a couple weeks ago, I didn't even know your last name. Or your first, for that matter."

"London is all the world needs to know."

"Okay."

"Where are we going?"

"Hiking."

"What?" she exclaimed, as though he'd said they were jumping off a cliff without parachutes.

He looked at her feet. "I told you to wear comfortable shoes."

"These are all I had."

He shrugged. "If I had Clarisse in the car, I'd stop and buy her a pair of Nikes. But since it's you, deal with it."

"You're a trip." She shook her head, then rested it against the headrest. "We need to stop anyway. I haven't eaten yet and I'm starved."

"All taken care of, baby. We'll eat soon." London looked over at the man who made her heartbeat increase and certain muscles clench and realized he was right. They'd spent much of their time doing instead of talking. But the more she knew about him, the more she wanted to know.

"How'd you get into modeling?"

"My high school art teacher trying to keep me out of trouble. She saw my drawings and thought I had potential, encouraged me to develop a couple designs

I'd played around with. I did, and afterward she sent them to a friend she knew in New York, along with a pic of me. He wasn't interested in my clothes but bought a plane ticket for me to come try out at a modeling agency. Next thing I knew, my parents were looking over contracts and hiring attorneys. I signed on and the agency secured me a tutor and an apartment in New York. Life took off from there."

"How old were you?"

"Fifteen."

This answer raised London's brow. "That's pretty young. I bet you were so excited, thought you were the man!"

"I was an insecure boy living in a man's body and a man's world. Until that year I felt anything but desirable. I was short, skinny, with legs, arms and a head too big for my body. Then I had a six-inch growth spurt, my voice deepened, I grew a hair or two—my whole body changed. But inside, I was still that jacked-up little kid. So the experience was scarier than I would ever have admitted at the time. Some life lessons come much more quickly than they should."

"Give me a for instance."

"My tutor was a young twentysomething who had a sister. We were in the same grade and equally curious. She began to join him during my lessons. After he taught me equations in math and science, we went into the bedroom for lessons in anatomy."

"Knowing how you operate, you probably led the way."

"No. I talked a good game back then but didn't know nothing." He glanced at her and said a bit shyly, "She was my first."

"Did you get your degree?"

"Yes." He paused and then added, "In both classes."

He exited the highway, turned off a main street and continued up a curvy road that led into a park. Glimpses of the water as they'd made certain turns let London know they were close the ocean. It was a perfect day to be there. The sun shone bright and high in the sky, making it feel warmer than the sixty-one degrees the car thermostat registered. He turned off a main street and continued up a curvy road that led into a park.

"What's this park? I've never been here."

Ace smiled, seeming proud of himself that he'd treated her to something new. "It's called Lands End."

"That's a strange name."

"You'll see why when we finish our hike."

"Ace, I'm not hiking in these shoes."

"Yeah, I thought you'd try and punk out on me. But I'm prepared."

He jumped out of the car, went around to the trunk and came back with a canvas tote in one hand and a decorated recycled bag in the other. He got back inside.

"What is this?"

"Just open it, London."

With eyes still on him she slid back the zipper. Inside the tote was a pair of brand-new tennis shoes and a Windbreaker.

"These look like they'll fit." She removed her boots and put them on. Perfect. "How'd you know my size?"

"You're the head model for our women's couture line. I know everything about you."

London chuckled. "You know next to nothing."

But looking out for her like that? Good move.

"What's in the other bag?"

Instead of answering her, he exited the car, came around to her side and opened the door. "Let's go."

"I guess you're not going to tell me."

"No, you'll have to wait."

He locked the car and took her hand. For the next half hour she followed his lead. He took them to the water's edge, past the ruins of a nineteenth-century Victorian bathhouse and through a tunnel where echoes of water crashing against rocks bounced off the stone walls. When they reached a stairway toward the California Coastal Trail, London was thankful for sneakers. The hike up was steep but not overly arduous. A walk through a grove of cypress trees led to a labyrinth and craggy bluffs with stunning thirty-mile views of the Golden Gate Bridge, Marin Headlands and the city. The picturesque scene before her and the inventive man beside her made it well worth the climb. Ace's thinking, she discovered, was much like his company's name—definitely out of the box.

She wandered over to a cliff facing the bridge, closed her eyes and took a deep breath. It had been a long time since she'd been this physical outside of bed. Blessed with a fast metabolism and good genes, London had a naturally high energy level and never watched what she ate. Back in high school, she'd begrudgingly participated in sports. That was probably the last time she'd done anything that came close to the hike they'd just made up the mountain. Though Ace was probably a factor, she reasoned, the strenuous walk was the cause of her rapid heartbeat, the exhilaration of simply being alive.

"Clarisse."

She turned around. Her breath caught. Heartbeats increased. Ace had found a plot of grass and removed the contents of the bag he carried. Two boxed lunches sat on a plastic tablecloth, along with a bottle of sparkling water, a bowl of fruit and two plastic cups. She looked from the modest spread to the man who'd prepared it, caught the challenging yet vulnerable look in his eyes. She saw the jacked-up little boy he'd described the other night thrown into a world of wolves. And for the first time in a long time she imagined someone's feelings above her own.

She walked to stand in front of him, raised up for a quick kiss. "I've eaten in the finest restaurants in exotic places all over the world. But by far, this is sure to be my favorite meal."

She watched his eyes shift from conveying worry to relief. He pulled her into an embrace. They kissed until her nipples pebbled and she felt his erection stirring.

Ace pulled away. "There's a choice of turkey on wheat, pastrami on sourdough or a vegetarian wrap. For dessert—" he reached up and trailed a finger down the side of her face "—I'd like something caramel."

"Then I say we get started." London sat cross-legged on the cloth and pulled a bottle of sanitizer out of her bag. The sooner they devoured the sandwiches, the sooner they could have dessert. And since it was clear Ace was the adventurous, outdoorsy type, she hoped they wouldn't have to get all the way back to the city to enjoy it.

She didn't have to wait.

On the way back to the car, once inside the tunnel, he took her hand and led them behind a jutting rock. No need to ask what was on his mind. His eyes were black with desire, his hard shaft imprinted against her thigh. She was equally hot for him. Something about being outside, technically in public, added another level of thrill. He settled against the tunnel wall, pulling her with him. Lined her lips with his tongue, kissed her cheeks and temples.

"You don't mind, do you?" he whispered against her ear.

"Mind?"

"Yeah. Making this little pit stop before heading back into the city."

London looked him in the eye as she reached for his belt buckle. "You can make a stop like this anytime you want."

She wrapped a hand around his manhood. He groaned, raised her sweater and pulled a nipple into his mouth. The move brought moisture to London's pearl, made her crazy with wanting to have him inside her. She pulled off her leggings. Shivered from the cold, but not for long. Ace soon filled her with the heat of his desire. Made the goose bumps disappear. Made her forget about everything except this moment, this meeting of the minds and melding of bodies. Soft moans and increased pelvic movements signaled her approaching release. Waves crashed against the water as Ace caught her scream in a kiss. He held her close and let go, too. Then kissed her with such tenderness that she could have wept.

They dressed quickly, reached the car as thunderclouds swirled and the temperature dipped. Leaving Lands End, London had a new appreciation for hiking—and a deeper appreciation for the man who'd brought her here.

Chapter 16

London arrived back in Paradise Cove on Sunday afternoon just in time for brunch and a house full of Drakes. In other words, just in time for Operation Interrogation. From the number of cars parked in the circular driveway, it looked like every sibling, spouse and child had decided to show up today. And wouldn't you know it? In her hasty departure she'd forgotten the side-door key that would have let her sneak in unnoticed. She'd have to go through the front door. Great.

The car stopped just beyond the main entrance. As she refused his offer for help with her luggage and gave him a generous tip, London tried to convince herself of the slight chance that only Quinn had seen the latest tabloid headlines. Her sister, Teresa, had a blog and was always online. No doubt she'd seen it. That meant Teresa's twin brother, Terrell, knew. And if he knew, so did Niko. Heck, all of the siblings had probably read the stories. Had they kept their mouths shut? London had her doubts.

By the time she reached the front door, she'd changed her mind about facing the questioning head-on and opted to try to make it to her room unnoticed. Hide out until the brunch munchers left. Talking to her parents without the familial judge and jury present would offer the chance for more damage control.

Opening the front door slowly, she removed her shoes and tipped into the foyer and over to the double staircase closest to her wing. Laughter spilled from the formal dining room along with the clanking of silver on china. Her hopes grew. The noisy clan's antics might have covered the sound of the car. She placed a foot on the first step and prayed there would be no creaking.

First step. Silence. Yes!

Second step, the tricky one. A little creak, not much.

"London? Is that you?"

London could have sworn Jennifer had hall video monitors behind her eyeballs. There was no way she could have heard that tiny creak all the way in the dining room. Especially over the raucous voices coming from there.

She thought about not answering but knew that was useless. Jennifer would just employ a sibling or two to smoke her out of hiding. She slunk down the stairs, resigned to her fate. Putting on a brave face and a runway walk, she entered the dining room. "Hey, everybody!"

A small cacophony of greetings erupted from almost a dozen Drakes seated around the massive custom-made platinum, glass and mahogany table. No children were present. The nannies no doubt were with the next generation in a former sitting room on the other side of the house that had been turned into a playroom paradise.

So far, so good. No cheeky comments or sly innuendos. Maybe her family had become immune to the tabloids. Like she had. She hoped so. One of the things she hoped to do during this time at home was reestablish the type of bond with her parents she saw her siblings enjoy. That would be much easier if she didn't have to explain dancing in a club with a bare-butt cowboy. She kissed her mom and dad, who sat at opposite ends of the table, before continuing to the food-laden buffet that anchored the far wall, filling a bowl with fresh fruit, placing a bagel on a saucer and taking the empty chair next to Terrell to enjoy her first course.

She'd barely bitten into her first juicy strawberry when the query began.

Jennifer led the way. "How was San Francisco, dear?"

London nodded as she swallowed her bite. "Good. Great, actually. In fact, I've got news."

This quieted the chatter all around. She felt like Tupac. All eyes on her.

"I thought we'd have to pull the news out of you," Ike Jr. said, eyes slightly judging.

London caught Quinn's subtle eye warning. Ike Jr. knew. Dang it. Suddenly she wished her glass of orange juice were a mimosa. Though what the tabloids treated like breaking news was really no big deal, her father and his namesake bristled at any hint of controversy. The faster she explained what happened, the faster they could move on. So she dived right in.

"What? The picture of me dancing with Mr. Tuxedo and the bare-butt cowboy?"

Ike Sr. choked on his water. Some laughed. Others scowled. Jennifer's expression remained placid. She'd weathered worse storms.

Warren, who along with wife, Charli, owned a ranch and vineyard, was the first to comment in a string of many. "And here I thought you weren't too fond of the ranch life."

"Wait a minute. I didn't see the picture, just read the article. A man actually showed his bare behind?" Niko asked.

"He wasn't totally naked. He had on chaps," Teresa said.

Monique chimed in, "You can't take a story like that at face value. Especially when it comes from *XYZ*."

"Just please tell me that's not part of OTB's new line," Terrell joked.

London gave him a playful jab. "You're silly."

Quinn tried to make light of the matter. "It was San Francisco, you guys, where everything goes and anything can happen."

Ike Jr. slid her a glance. "Thanks for letting me know. I'll be sure next time to send along a bodyguard—me."

"You took that the wrong way! What happens isn't necessarily wrong or bad. And what was taking place when that picture was taken is nothing like what the articles implied."

Ike Sr. spoke through a scowl. "Exactly what did happen, Clarisse?"

She gave them the short version, mainly the whispered conversation that allowed the questionable photograph. "It's a private club," she finished. "A neighborhood hangout where most are regulars and everyone knows everybody else. I was actually surprised paparazzi was there."

"So were they," Quinn added. "Trent said the owner was very upset. Especially when he learned that a member, not paparazzi had taken the photo. When they find out who leaked that photograph, his membership will be revoked."

"Does someone have the picture?" Jennifer asked. "I'd like to see it. But not now," she hurriedly added. "It doesn't seem appropriate for the dinner table. Later, Teresa, send me a link. My question was strictly about your work with OTB and whether or not you had a chance to talk with the designer about our charity event."

"I'm sorry, Mom. The weekend was so hectic I completely forgot. I can tell you that for the next two weeks nothing but fashion week will be on their minds. I will mention it to Ace, though, I promise. Everyone breathes a little easier after the first show. I'll bring it up to him when we're in New York."

Ike Sr.'s frown had diminished as London retold the incidents of last Thursday. Her talk of travel brought it back. "New York? You promised your mother and me that you'd take a break from modeling, spend some time at home to reconnect with your family."

"I am, Daddy. I mean, I will. Before coming home for Papa Dee's funeral, I had my agent totally clear my schedule for the next three months."

"Then what happened?"

"Ace showed up in Temecula," her brother interjected.

London's head swiveled around to Terrell. "How'd you know?"

"I've got connections, sis. Remember that."

London whacked his arm, looked past him at his wife, Aliyah. "Help me out, Ali. How did he know?"

Aliyah laughed at Terrell's glare before answering. "He talked to Dexter."

"Traitor," Terrell mumbled.

"Hey, I've got to stay true to the sisterhood."

"You're supposed to stay true to me."

"He has a point, Aliyah," Jennifer said. Terrell's chest swelled. "The proper action would have been to remain quiet and demure while next to your husband and share that information later, when you and Clarisse were alone."

A mixture of laughs, groans and pushback filled the

room. Jennifer picked up her tea, nice and ladylike, and took a sip. Above the rim, she winked in Aliyah and London's direction. Women unite!

"Is that true?" Niko asked. "The owner of OTB was at the resort?"

London nodded. "Just for a couple days, to get away from the stress of fashion week."

"And he ran into you," Ike said, shaking his head. "Poor fella."

Everybody laughed at that, even London. Obviously Terrell and Quinn knew about it but for some family members her being the face of Ace's new line was news.

Charli got up for seconds and headed to the buffet. "I don't get it. If he makes menswear, why does he need you?"

"That news will hit the public later today, if it hasn't already. OTB is introducing a women's line. I will serve as the spokesperson."

Jennifer's eyes beamed. "Really, honey? I thought you were just doing the fashion shows. Sounds fantastic. But it also sounds like a lot of work."

"Sounds like you're going back on your word," Ike Sr. intoned.

"Just moving the date a little, Dad. One of the conditions in accepting the spokesperson position was that as much shooting as possible could happen during the four-week period of fashion week's major shows. The rest will be done either in San Francisco or here."

"Now you're talking," Niko said. "At times I've wondered whether or not you were dropped off on the doorstep. But bringing positive attention and possible revenue to the city is a definite Drake move."

"Thank you, Mr. Mayor."

"Good heavens, Clarisse. In hearing about your tabloid piece I forgot breaking news. Diamond had her baby!"

"What? When? How am I just now finding out?"

"It happened while you were in transit, and quite quickly. Genevieve said she's exhausted as can be expected, but Mommy and baby Jackson are doing fine."

Jennifer stood and continued. "Ladies, would you all like to join me for a short jaunt to walk off that massive meal?"

"Guys, you know what that means," Ike said. "We're getting ready to be the topic of conversation."

"No, you're safe this week," Jennifer replied as she stood. "The topic of this walk is going to be Ace Montgomery."

London groaned as she got up to join the ladies as they made their exit. She was willing to tell all when it came to business and the daytime hours. But about what happened once the lights went out...her lips were sealed.

Chapter 17

For Ace, the next two weeks flew by. He'd barely had time to text London, let alone call and talk to her. Seeing her was out of the question. The PR blitz had filled the week after her trip to San Francisco, and for the past week he and a team of twenty from OTB had been in New York. All the work had paid off. OTB Her, and more specifically London, was a topic on every major fashion- or entertainment-oriented website, blog and TV show.

The photo now simply known as "the shot" had been blown up to gargantuan proportions and occupied prime real estate above Times Square. The picture was magical and mystical all at once. While the image had been enhanced, as all fashion pics were, the burst of light and lightning highlighting London's face and rain-drenched skin was totally real and amazing. The fashion world had come calling, as the partners had predicted. They'd moved the show to a larger venue and had been offered a prime-time Friday-night slot.

The flurry of activity had left Ace little time to contact London. But it hadn't kept her off his mind. Finally, last night, he couldn't take it anymore. Technically she wasn't needed in town for another three days, but Ace had instructed his team to try and get her in early. He'd had a flood of invitations since getting into town and figured attending the events with her would generate great publicity. That's what he told the team, anyway. And it was true. But the OTB Her line wasn't the main reason he'd had London summoned. The main reason was because he missed her. His days didn't seem as bright without her in them.

Frida came into Ace's temporary office. He was on the phone, but before she was fully in the room he'd placed the call on hold. "Is she coming?"

"It took some crazy coordination, but we managed to get her from Paradise Cove to San Francisco and on a nonstop flight that left just before noon. She gets in to JFK at eight twenty tonight."

"First class, right?"

"Absolutely."

"Make sure there's a car waiting for her at the airport and assign a personal assistant for whatever she might need. You said eight thirty?"

"About that time. I'd say by the time we get her baggage and allow for traffic, she'll be in the city around ten."

"Crap."

"What is it, Ace?"

"I didn't even think about her lodging. I bet all the suites are taken."

"I knew you'd be too busy to think about it, boss, but I did. Booked the Prestige suite for her when I booked yours two weeks ago."

"Frida, you just earned your bonus."

"And an extra three days in New York with the hotel on the company?"

"Don't push it."

London arrived at the hotel a little after ten. But she didn't see her suite that night. After a late dinner with Ace, publicists, editors from the world's top fashion magazines and hosts of a top TV show doing an exclusive on OTB Her, he pulled her finger away from the button to her floor and took them straight to his penthouse suite.

The next morning, Ace awoke to London's soft lips on his hard shaft. He'd missed more than their sexual escapades, but this good-morning convinced him their romps ran a close second to whatever was first.

"Baby," he gritted between clenched teeth. "We've got a busy day ahead."

Her eyes floated up over his erection. "All the more reason to begin it with a good workout."

The next three days were a blur. The Times Square billboard had gotten the attention of the entire city. London was booked on all the major talk shows. Even Ace, who preferred to remain behind the scenes, was pulled into the spotlight. When he wasn't doing publicity or making last-minute changes to the fashion show outfits or line up, he was in the suite with London, rubbing feet now sore from practicing the grand finale walk in two-foot stilts.

Finally, showtime. Ace left the backstage flurry to Lucien and his capable crew. He took up a position near the runway entrance, waiting on his cue to announce the line. Most designers would be nervous at this time. But it was in this moment—with the crowd buzzing, the music pulsating, the back room a frenzy of models in various states of undress—that Ace became calm. He looked out at the audience, and though the lights prevented him from seeing her, imagined his mom and her best friend in the fifth row. His eyes scanned the front rows, where the stars were clearly visible. The huge rapper and his reality-star wife. The talk-show mogul and her lifelong BFF. The young pop artist topping the charts and the record executive who'd discovered her. The NBA star and his too-live crew. Just as the coordinator signaled that they were about to begin, Ace noticed someone else—Maxwell Tata.

"One minute, Mr. Montgomery."

Ace didn't have time to react or to figure out which assistant he needed to fire. He straightened the cuffs on his tunic-style pantsuit, an original OTB design, and it was five, four, three, two...

"Good evening! Tonight it is my honor to present an idea several years in the making. Clothes not just for any woman, but for those who think outside the box. These designs were inspired by women like my mother—strong, fierce, exquisite—and like the well-known woman closing out this show. The wait is over. Introducing Out of the Box's new creation, OTB Her!"

Seconds after the music changed, London burst through the curtain. The wide-legged jumpsuit covering her body came alive as she walked on nine-inch wooden wedge heels that closely resembled the two-foot stilts she'd wear at the end. The wedges were one of the show's signatures, worn by all the models. But none of them walked in them quite like London did. She reached the end of the runway and became almost robotic in her movements. The crowd broke out in applause. Ace watched as even the jaded celebrities clapped and cheered. London's star quality couldn't be taught, rarely even honed by those with the best intentions.

Eighteen looks followed London's strong beginning: suits, dresses, separates, coats. Then it was time for the finale. They'd rehearsed it several times. Ace was convinced it would go off without a hitch. But he was nervous. A lot was involved.

The music changed. Sounds of thunder rumbled through the building. Special bulbs caused lightning to flicker across the stage and throughout the room. London crouched behind a screen that made her appear twenty feet tall. A murmur ran through the crowd. She stood. The crowd went wild. The lion's mane of hair that had been pinned up in previous walks now swung past her backside. She came around the curtain on two-foot stilts, walking on them like they were the Nikes she'd worn on the trail. Camera flashes shot off from every direction. The crowd followed her as with one set of eyes. She reached the center of the runway, stopped and posed. It was unexpected. The customary walk for all models was all the way to the end. A Plexiglas cylinder dropped from the rafter. A collective gasp. And then came the rain. Thunder. Lightning. And London, expertly recreating the look that was plastered all over the world.

Standing ovation. The show was a wrap. In that second, OTB became the star of fashion week.

Ace snaked through the packed backstage crowd with determined strides. He reached his destination, picked London up from where she sat and slowly twirled them around.

"You were amazing," he whispered, uncaring of the flashes going off around them. "You've not only put OTB Her on top. You've changed the runway game."

"It was your vision," London said, eyes beaming.

Ace knew the adrenaline was still pumping. Shows like this were a model's dream.

"London, over here!"

"Excuse me, Ace, can I get a photo of you two together?"

"That ending was genius!"

Ace tried to field as many questions as possible. A firm arm kept London close to his side. Frida slipped him a note. He read it and nodded.

"Let's get you changed," he whispered to London. "100 Proof and other investors are hosting a celebration party. They're waiting for us."

A small skirmish caused Ace to turn around. A large bodyguard pushed his way through the crowd. Behind him was the man Ace had forgotten about until this moment.

"There she is!"

London turned, too, and was swept into a hug before she could react. "Max!"

Strong arms pulled her away from the director. Ace placed one of those arms around London's waist and challenged Max with his eyes, but said nothing.

Max looked at Ace in surprise, as though just realizing he was standing there. Just as quickly he dismissed him.

"London, you were incredible! Sweetheart, the world is your oyster. I've already been on the phone. Where are your things? Let's go. I've got some people I want you to meet."

"Sorry, Max. I've got plans."

"I assure you they're not bigger than mine. Come on, limo's waiting."

Ace took a step toward Maxwell. London hurriedly stepped between them. "I've got appearances, Max. Let's talk later, okay?"

Maxwell continued to ignore Ace. "Sure, sweetheart." He leaned to plant a kiss on her mouth. She turned her face. He caught a cheek. "I always knew you'd shine on the stage as well as the runway." He turned to walk away, his goon behind him. "Call me when you finish tonight. I'll send a car for you to join me on the Upper East Side."

Ace watched Maxwell and his King Kong sideman disappear into the crowd. He pulled out his phone and sent a text to Tyler to remove the director's name from the invite list for all future shows. Any questions about what type of relationship Ace wanted with London had just been answered. He wanted them to be exclusive, and Maxwell Tata was the first person who needed to know.

Chapter 18

Tyler and his husband, Phillip, met Ace and London as they were whisked through a side door.

Tyler waylaid him. "You don't want Maxwell Tata, practically Hollywood friggin' royalty, at the shows? What the hell happened?"

Both Tyler and London awaited Ace's answer as the couples slid into the waiting limo.

"I don't want him around."

Tyler looked at London, who shrugged, and back to Ace. "I don't get it, man. Press follows wherever he goes. There's even opportunity for our clothes to be worn in his movies. Or by his next blockbuster movie's leading lady, or—"

"Look, I just don't like him, all right? He's seen the show. Anything else he wants to know about the line he can find online. I want that ban enforced, Dent, you got that? No team vote on this one. I've made up my mind."

Tyler shook his head but said nothing further, just slunk back in the cushy leather seats, quietly grabbed his husband's hand and watched Manhattan go by. Ace knew he'd been borderline rude to his partner. He'd even entertain the notion that his intense dislike for Maxwell Tata was unwarranted. All he knew about the guy was that he made movies and had dated London, who didn't seem to have a problem with him coming around. Why was he so bothered? Sure, he didn't like Maxwell's obsession with London but it was more than that. He didn't like Maxwell, but that wasn't it either. Ace couldn't explain the uncomfortable feeling. Nor could he shake it. Until he could do one or the other, he intended to keep up his guard.

After another moment of silence, London kissed his cheek and whispered, "You okay?"

He reached for her hand. "Better now."

"Don't let whatever happened back there ruin this moment. It was a long time coming. Try to enjoy it."

Ace squeezed her hand. He took a deep breath, brought her hand up and kissed it.

"Sorry about my earlier attitude, man," Ace said to Tyler. "I shouldn't have snapped at you."

Tyler waved off the apology. "Don't worry about it."

"I owe you an explanation."

"Another time. Tonight's for celebrating!"

"It sure is," Phillip exclaimed, reaching for a bottle of Dom Pérignon. "For a second there I thought we were in a funeral procession. This is supposed to be a no-holds-barred bash!"

Tyler reached over to the bar and handed everyone a flute. "Hey, I just thought about Mira. Where is she?"

"Already at the venue."

"Oh, okay. Babe, will you do the honors?" Phillip

filled the glasses. Tyler looked at Ace with a sober expression. "When you suggested a women's line two years ago, I thought you were crazy." He lifted his glass. "Now I'm sure of it!"

Laughter, clinking glasses and shouts of cheer rang out.

"To London," Ace said, "the reason everyone's talking."

"Don't sell yourself short," London replied. "You're the reason I'm here."

By the time the limo stopped in front of their destination, Ace's good mood had been fully restored. Stars, an exclusive club on Manhattan's Upper East Side, was where celebrities, investors and the fashion world's elite had been invited to celebrate OTB Hers's incredible launch success.

At first Ace had balked at the idea of bodyguards, but seeing the crowd blocking the club's entrance, he was now glad for the three who'd followed in the car behind. Now the men whisked them out of the limo and cleared a path through the throng of reporters, photographers and star watchers so Ace and company could get inside. Mira spotted the group as soon as they came through the club's inner doors.

She hurried to the stage and spoke into the microphone. "May I have your attention, please? Everyone, please help me welcome my partners, Tyler Dent and Ace Montgomery, along with London, the face of OTB Her!"

Amid boisterous applause, Ace held London's hand as they made their way through the crowd, him shaking hands, her giving hugs, both accepting pats on the back. Eyes filled with curiosity darted between him and London. Neither missed these speculative glances. Ace imagined the world would dub them a couple by morning, whether it was true or not.

They reached the slightly elevated stage area and accepted flutes of bubbly from Mira. Ace placed an arm around London and brought her close to his side. She cocked her head toward him, her expression partly inquisitive, partly amused. He noticed but couldn't help it. Ace had fallen head over heels for a runway star with a pretty face, a pert behind and a smart mouth. Tomorrow he'd regain his serious composure and place their relationship back in the private box where it belonged. But tonight...

The crowd of more than two hundred well-wishers continued to clap and cheer. Ace stepped to the microphone. "Thank you! Thanks, everyone." The din lowered to a murmur as he continued to speak. "On behalf of my partners, Tyler Dent and Mira Jacobs, we want to thank all of you for embracing this new line so enthusiastically. The world's a fickle place, nowhere more so than the entertainment and fashion industries. So we didn't know what to expect. Back in the warehouse amid the designs, especially when we saw them on London, we knew these out-of-the-box fashions were a hit. But I can't tell you how good it feels to know you feel that way, too. Here's to the launch and to London, the face of the brand and the woman who first made the clothes come alive... To OTB Her!"

Once again, there were toasts all around. Ace put the glass to his lips but didn't imbibe. Not much of a drinker, he'd passed his one-drink limit three drinks ago in the limo. Reporters clamored near the side of the stage. He'd not planned a press conference but decided to call on a couple raised hands.

"Any plans to expand the line beyond clothing?"

London squeezed Ace's hand, hard. "As of right now, everything is on the table. We're always thinking outside the box."

"Whose idea was it to incorporate stilts into the show? That was fantastic!"

Tyler stepped up to the microphone. "As with the line, the show's design was a collaborative effort."

Actually it was Ace's idea, but given the bully he'd been in the limo, Ace gave him a pass.

"You two look awfully cozy," a gossip columnist asked as she stepped to the front. "Is there perhaps some designing happening behind the scenes?"

London took the lead on this one. "What fun would it be to kiss and tell? Part of the excitement for you guys is chasing the story." She added coyly, "If I were you, I'd keep running."

More questions were shouted out. Mira stepped to the microphone. "That's all the time we have for questions right now. It's time to meet and greet all of you who've come to help us celebrate. We appreciate you beyond words. Now…let's party!"

For the next several hours, that's exactly what they did. At just before 2:00 a.m., the partners and their partners arrived back at the Baccarat. Inside the elevator, Ace tried to stop her, but London pushed the button for her floor.

"You know better than that," he murmured, using his body to press hers against the wall. "In fact," he continued, kissing her cheeks, eyes, lips, "if we weren't leaving in two days, I'd have Frida cancel the reservation altogether. There's no way I'm going to bed without you in it."

"You'll get no argument out of me. But I need to stop at my room and grab a few things." They reached her floor. The elevator doors opened. "Coming with?"

"Sure, why not."

London playfully fought Ace off her as they walked down the hall. It was as if he'd channeled an octopus and now had eight hands. When he tried to put a hand under her dress while simultaneously tweaking a breast, London ran to her door.

"No more champagne for you, Mr. Montgomery. You've lost all control!"

They were both laughing as she swiped the card and the door opened. Two steps inside the foyer, however, Ace's smile slid away. There, on the dining room table, was one of the largest bouquets Ace had ever seen, and beside it, gift boxes.

"Oh!" London squealed. "Flowers!" Her eyes beamed as she looked at him.

Ace shook his head. "Not me."

"Are you sure?"

They walked over to the massive arrangement. London searched for and found the card.

To the star of the runway, and the world. You light up my life. Your one and only…

Ace read the card over her shoulder. "Looks like I pegged it right at the warehouse. You might be over Max, but he's not over you."

"This isn't from Max," London replied, thoughtfully nibbling on her lip as she picked up two wrapped packages. "There's nothing he does that doesn't bear his name."

She unwrapped the first package. A box of gourmet chocolates. Unwrapped the second. A sheer negligee.

"Are you sure this isn't from you?" London asked,

trying to add levity to a moment getting heavier by the second.

"Positive. Are you sure they aren't from Max?"

"Ninety-nine percent positive."

"Call him and make sure."

"Let me get this straight. The same man you banned from future shows you now want me to contact?"

"Yes, as quickly as possible. It's the second time this has happened in as many months. Right? Or have there been more?"

"No, just the other time in Temecula."

"Yes, call him. I don't like the feel of this."

"It's probably nothing more than an overzealous fan."

"Who knows where you've traveled, and where you stay?"

"Papa Dee's funeral announcement was in several papers. Maybe someone made a lucky guess."

He made further points that she continued to counter. Partly, he knew, because she wanted these to be random coincidences, not signs of something ominous. She'd tried to make light of the situation, but he knew the truth. Could see it in her eyes. She didn't like the feel of it, either.

Chapter 19

"I didn't send anything."

London walked out of the bedroom of her suite and into the kitchen. Her voice was light but low. "That's not the answer I wanted to hear, Max, but it's what I figured."

"Why's that, my love? When we were together I sent you tons of flowers."

"Yes, and you always signed your name."

It was the following morning. London was in her suite at the Baccarat, along with Carly, the woman OTB had paid to be her personal assistant for the next four weeks. They were packing up for London, England, the next leg of the tour. Their flight left later today.

"It shouldn't surprise you to have a secret admirer or two...or twelve."

"It's weird, though. A couple weeks ago, a gift was delivered to where I was in Temecula. A personal event that was announced, but that I hadn't publicized anywhere."

"It's very easy to get information these days. You know that."

"I guess. It still feels uncomfortable to have someone know your whereabouts when you don't know who they are."

"Our business attracts weird people, baby. It's probably harmless, some shy geek millionaire garnering the courage to approach you. Sounds like some nice gifts, though. I'd enjoy them."

"You're probably right. Thanks. I feel better."

"When you're around me, you always do. Speaking of which, I'll be in Europe in a week or so and plan to catch your show. But my contact couldn't get a ticket. Says there aren't any left."

None left for you. "That's probably true, Max. We were all over the trade mags and websites. Everyone's talking about OTB."

"No, princess. They're talking about you. That star quality I saw the first time we met." His tone changed, softened. London's discomfort increased.

"I miss you, London. Your breaking things off was a huge mistake. I was so angry back then, had put so much into your being in the next movie, the next Tata temptation. I said things that I shouldn't have, things I didn't mean. When I saw you at the show Friday night, it became clearer than ever that you're meant for the spotlight, and you're meant to be with me."

"Max… I don't know what to say to all of this. We broke up months ago, and we only dated a year. I've moved on."

"With Ace Montgomery?"

"With life, Max."

"I take that nonanswer to mean you are seeing him."

"Ace and I are very good friends, but no, we're not officially a couple."

"And unofficially?"

"Right now I'm taking a break from everything, taking the time to get to know my family again, to know me again. I told you that before. It's still true."

"Yet you're headed to London for the next show."

"Max, there are dozens, no, hundreds of beautiful women who'd kill to be your next temptation. The timing is just not right for that girl to be me. I have to go finish packing. Take care of yourself, okay?"

"Get me a ticket for your show in Paris."

"I don't have anything to do with that, Max."

"I saw the look in Ace's eyes. He'll do anything for you. One ticket. That's all I'm asking."

"I'll see what I can do."

London ended the call, shaking her head. Men. Who could ever understand them? After breaking up with him, Max had understandably tossed her from his Hollywood mansion. A message that she'd never get anywhere in the town without him was his parting gift, along with the fact it had been in the middle of the night. He'd apologized later, and they'd agreed to be friends. Platonic. Cordial. And now he was chasing her across the pond and declaring his love? What was that about?

Several hours later London joined Ace, Tyler and Phillip, Mira and her husband, along with Lucien and his top two assistants on a private plane to London. She hadn't seen Ace since they parted that morning, but no sooner had they buckled up than it became clear what was on his mind.

"You talk to him?"

"Yes."

"Did he send them?"

"No."

"Temecula, either?"

"Nope."

"Do you believe him?"

London looked over. "Why would he lie?"

"I don't know."

"He didn't send them, Ace. If he had, trust me, I would know."

Mira leaned over. "What are you guys over there conspiring about?"

Ace stretched his long legs out in front of him. "Just casual conversation, Mira. No story to feed to the press."

"Are you sure about that? You two definitely look good together. Don't they, Phillip?"

Phillip readily agreed. "They make a striking couple."

"No couple," London offered.

Mira continued to study them. "We need to shoot you guys together. What do you think, Ty? Coordinating the two lines for the spring show?"

Tyler yawned. "I think we need to relax, maybe sleep and not think about work on this flight. There'll be plenty of time to plan the spring rollout after we get through the fall."

"I agree, Dent," Ace said. "One step at time."

Mira huffed. "You two are no fun at all."

"Says the workaholic," her husband offered.

"You'd best behave," Mira warned. "Or there will be a one-way coach ticket on a cheap airline with your name on it."

The plane leveled off. Shortly afterward, dinner orders were taken and drinks were served.

London took a sip of her cranberry juice and nudged Ace. He lifted his head from the headrest and opened his eyes.

"I've been meaning to ask you something."

"What?"

"Do you remember getting a request to put on a fashion show for charity?"

Ace thought for a minute. "Not that I can recall. Why?"

"My mom belongs to a few social organizations, one of which raises money for various causes. She said someone reached out to several designers in hopes of putting on a show to raise money for this year's recipients."

"When did they send it?"

"A month ago, maybe? Probably when you were in the throes of fashion week prep."

"For sure, anything that came across my desk in the last two months, other than what pertained to the line, was placed in a file to be looked at later. I'm always down for a good cause, though. Tell me more."

"I don't know much, really, other than that all of the recipients are in Paradise Cove and one of them is the Drake Community Center. They have a variety of programs for kids, especially those who are at risk of falling through the cracks." When he remained silent, she turned to find him staring. "Why are you looking at me like that?"

"The more I learn about you and your family, the more you intrigue me. Let me make sure I understand. Your enormously wealthy family runs a multimillion-dollar real estate company, operates a luxury resort and vineyard, and at the same time built a community center for at-risk kids."

"Basically, although if you'll remember the spa is owned by my first cousins, not us. We do have a vineyard in Paradise Cove, but it's a small one that my rancher brother runs."

"Wait, wait, wait. There's a rancher, too? I can't keep up."

"Ha! It's my normal, so I never think about it. I come from a big family. We have a lot going on."

The flight attendant delivered the first course. Ace had opted for the beet and goat cheese salad, while London tasted a spoonful of her chilled asparagus soup.

"Tell me about your siblings. Are they as wild as you?"

"I'm not wild. Much. Though if asked, they'd agree with you. My sister, Teresa, is the good girl. I've always been the rebel."

"No question whether or not you're the youngest. Wreaking havoc because you got here last."

"Ha!"

"Tell me about the others."

"The oldest is named after our father, Ike. He heads up Drake Realty Plus and is married to Quinn, the one who met me in San Francisco and who you would have met if you weren't so busy. The next oldest is Niko. He's the mayor of Paradise Cove."

Ace snickered.

"What?"

"Go on, I'm listening."

"Don't laugh at my family. Drakes don't play that."

"I'm not laughing at you, babe. It's just that you're mentioning all of these serious corporate and government positions. And then there's you."

She nudged him in the side. "Watch it."

"Then there's Reginald, who's the real rebel. He married his soul mate, moved to New Orleans and became the son her father never had. He's the only brother who doesn't work in the family business. Warren is the rancher, who started this whole conversation. He also works at Drake Realty. Everybody does something at the company in one way or another. Well, almost everybody."

"Except you, right."

"Dang, hearing it out loud makes me feel bad about it. You've got to do the show for my mom. I'll help. It'll be my contribution to the good Drake name."

They both laughed at that and took a break from the conversation to accept plates of wild Alaskan salmon and Chateaubriand.

"So now, the rancher. Is he married?"

London nodded. "Everyone is except me and Julian. He's the youngest son and just graduated with his doctorate in psychology. Let's see, who else. Oh, the twins, Terrell and Teresa. Terrell handles sales at the company and helps run the community center. His wife is a doctor, too. I forget which kind. Teresa worked for the company but took a leave, became a journalist, went to Alaska and met her husband. She's back in the family biz, but from home and part-time."

"Wow, babe. You're really lucky. Everyone in your family is highly educated, and very successful. They sound amazing. Whatever made you leave them to attend school in another country?"

"That's another story for another time. I'd rather talk about what type of fashion show we can put on for charity, and how much money we can make."

"Hell, sounds like we can just invite your family, have you walk the runway and make a mint!"

By the time the plane landed in London, one situation—the charity fashion show—had been all but worked out. Another situation was brewing, however, that might not turn out, as well.

Chapter 20

Once they landed at Heathrow Airport, London turned on her phone and was surprised to see several missed calls from her mother. They'd just spoken before the plane took off in New York. Her stomach flip-flopped. What could Jennifer want that she'd called so many times? London didn't bother to check messages, just tapped her mom's icon on the cell phone screen.

"Mom! Sorry to wake you. We just landed and I saw that I missed several calls. Is everything okay?"

"Absolutely, dear" was the groggy reply.

"Thank goodness." London breathed a sigh of relief. "Seeing so many calls almost stopped my heart. Especially since we'd talked earlier."

"I'm sorry to have frightened you, Clarisse. I was just so excited about my mini miracle that I wanted to contact you right away."

"What happened?"

"I got your father to not only take off from work but to do something that wasn't written on his calendar. He's agreed to come to Europe with me, sweetheart, to see one of your shows!"

London's squeal got the whole plane's attention. "Mommy, that's fabulous news! Are you coming to London? Milan? Where?"

"Well, honey, that's why I called you. I was hoping you could send me your schedule so that I can make plane reservations as soon as possible, before he changes his mind. I didn't know if we could make it in time for the London show, and then there's the matter of tickets and all of that. I just wanted to talk to you before I did anything further."

"Hold on, Mom. Ace is right here. Let me ask about tickets." She turned and quickly shared what Jennifer had told her.

"It's your parents. Of course we'll get them in."

"Which city should I tell them?"

"I'd say either here or Milan. You know how Paris is—always another level of crazy."

"You're right." She unmuted the call. "Mom, the show here is the day after tomorrow, so you might want to shoot for Milan next week. That way I could free up my schedule a little bit and actually hang out with you guys. It's been forever since you've seen me in a runway show. I'm really excited you're coming. Plus, you'll get to meet Ace. He's agreed to do the charity fashion show, so you two can start to get acquainted."

"Excellent! I look forward to all and will contact our travel agent as soon as you send the dates."

Landing at Heathrow's private-jet hangar considerably shortened the time it took to leave the airport. Everyone sailed through customs with ease. Assistants were on hand to deal with the baggage. Ace and company were free to get right down to business. With the show happening in two days, they didn't have a moment to lose.

London waited until Ace finished speaking with the crew and then approached him. "I downloaded the itinerary the publicist sent. Are you coming with me for all of this?"

"I wish I could, London, but we've got to head straight to the venue. I just looked at the pics of what's been done so far. There's a lot of work to do."

"Where is it going to be?"

"At this funky, cool eighteenth-century throwback on the Thames, with views of the London Eye and Tower Bridge. It's usually rented out for weddings, large parties, stuff like that. But by tomorrow night the main floor of that massive stone edifice will be transformed into a showroom and the runway will replicate a London alley, complete with rain cylinder, ready for the now highly anticipated show closer…you."

He leaned in for a kiss.

She averted the attempt. "Hey, what's with all the PDA?"

"I can't help myself. Come on, Samantha is waiting for you."

"Your company publicist, right?"

"Yes. She wasn't in New York, but you met her at that first meeting at OTB. She's handling the European leg and will make sure you get through everything. Call your personal assistant, too, if you need her. We know this is a lot of work and want to make it as painless as possible. So be sure and ask for whatever you need, okay?"

"I'll remember you said that."

It was early afternoon in the Old Smoke. The skies were overcast and the traffic brisk. London hardly noticed the right-sided drivers and double-decker buses, so busy was she interacting on social media and responding to emails about New York's show and the gossip that ensued. A horn startled her from the task just in time to take in the wrought-iron gates of Buckingham Palace and two bobbies conversing beneath Big Ben. A wisp of a smile as the scene brought back memories of when she'd jumped on a police officer's horse and spent the next two hours convincing him not to put her in jail or worse—call her parents. She'd spent a lot of time in her namesake. Movies could be made about her wild teenage years. The more London thought about it, Milan was definitely the better choice for her parents' visit. Less chance of running into an escaped skeleton from her closet moonwalking down Abbey Road.

Forty-eight hours later, London owned London. The show had gone off without a hitch and there were no floral deliveries. The team flew to Milan, the third of the fashion-week calendar's four major shows, with nothing but more success on their minds.

They arrived at Il Caravaggio International Airport, a smaller strip near Bergamo that served intercontinental flights and private planes such as the one the OTB team had flown in on. A car was waiting to take them to Seven Star Galleria, a boutique hotel of just seven suites near one of the oldest malls in the world, Milan's Galleria Vittorio Emanuele II. They would only be in Italy for two days so rather than a home, Frida had booked them into the presidential suite of this boutique—quiet, private and close to the runway-show location.

London yawned loudly and rested her head on Ace's shoulder.

He wrapped his arm around her and shifted for her

comfort. "My poor baby. I know it's a grind, but it's almost over."

"I'm okay." Said through yet another yawn.

"I hear how okay you are. I think I'll contact Samantha and cancel today's interviews. You need sleep."

"You know what ballers and shot callers say about that."

"No, what?"

"You sleep when you're dead."

"Yeah, well, while working my show, you're going to rest and prolong that inevitable eternal get down, okay?"

London nestled into him. "I wanted to visit the castle."

Ace rested his chin atop her hair. "I thought about that place, too. Where you and I met all those years ago."

"I wonder if anyone bought it or whether it's still being rented out for ridiculous prices." Ace shrugged, said nothing. Wheels turned.

"How long are your parents going to be here?"

"They arrive tomorrow and leave the day after our show for a ten-day tour of Italy. They'll see Rome, Florence, Tuscany and a couple more places."

"Sounds like a whirlwind trip. I can't wait to meet them."

Their assistants had flown commercially earlier, taken the bulk of luggage to the hotel and given the room cards to the driver who met them at the airport. They bypassed the front desk and, still keeping up appearances, took the stairs to their side-by-side suites on the third floor.

"This is beautiful," London said, admiring the decor as they walked down the hall. "Feels like a place to spend a honeymoon."

Ace gave her a look.

"Not with you!"

"What?"

"Wait, that didn't sound right. What I meant is that wasn't a subtle hint or anything."

"Yeah, right."

London sped Ace's walk down the hall with a playful push. Somewhere over the past few weeks they'd settled into the easygoing rapport of, well, an old married couple. Neither of them realized or would have admitted it, but being in each other's presence was why they felt so good.

They reached London's door first. "This is me."

"Here, let me get that for you." He went to put the card key in the slot. The door was already open, just slightly ajar.

"What's the matter, Ace?"

"The door is open. Hello?" He placed an ear near the door and awaited an answer. None came. He eased the door open wider, stuck his head inside. "Hello? *Ciao?*" Then turned to London. "Wait here."

As he entered the room, there was no hesitation in Ace's stride.

"Dammit!"

London pushed the door fully open, entered the room and followed Ace's eyes to a package on the hallway table. Patriotic colors of red, white and blue suggested the parcel had been sent from the United States.

She went over to pick it up.

"Don't!"

"Why not?"

"Don't touch it. Don't pick it up. This is gone past the actions of a love-struck fan and into straight stalker status. Your door was open. Either the person broke in or was a hotel employee with a key." He pulled out his phone. "Carly, where are you? I need you in London's suite. Now."

Carly was there within seconds.

Ace jabbed at the package. "How did this get here?"

Carly's eyes widened. "I have no idea."

"The door was unlocked when we arrived. Do you have an idea about that?"

Carly shook her head. "No. I definitely closed the door behind me."

"Are you sure?" London asked.

"Positive."

London walked over to the package.

"Don't touch it, London."

"I'm not. I'm just seeing who it's from." She leaned over to read the label and crossed her arms as she turned, a smirk on her face. "I think we can calm down, Ace. This has to be someone with a sense of humor, a harmless prank."

"Why, who's it from?"

"Emma Phan." Ace didn't laugh. "*I'm a fan.* Get it?"

"I get the name. Just not the joke."

London talked Ace out of involving law enforcement but not out of questioning the doorman, concierge and front desk clerk. No one had handled anyone with a package nor seen anyone enter with package in hand. There were no cameras in the hotel lobby or hallways. The manager assured Ace he'd get to the bottom of the matter and report back first thing the following day. The package was given to the concierge unopened, with instructions to return it to its sender.

They headed back up to their floor.

"You need to move into my room."

"Ace, that's a bit drastic. Besides, with my parents coming over, it's not a good idea."

"Why not? They're not staying here."

"But knowing my mother, she'll want to stop by. Why

don't I just keep my things in the room and spend the nights with you, like always?"

They entered her suite. Ace looked around. Now that the mysterious package was gone, the room looked and felt normal. He came over to stand in front of her, placed a finger under her chin to look into her eyes. "I'm going to have Samantha reschedule your interviews around tomorrow's appearances, baller or not. You can get some sleep and have more time to spend with your parents. Okay?"

"If you insist. We have dinner reservations for eight o'clock. If you haven't heard from me by seven, come wake me up."

Three hours later, at seven fifteen, Ace knocked lightly on London's door. No answer.

He knocked again. Still nothing. Pulling out the extra card key to her room that he'd requested earlier when they talked to the front desk, he opened the door and went inside.

"Hey, baller! London!" He walked through the living room and down a short hallway. "Thought you didn't need to get any—"

Ace stopped in his tracks and stopped talking, too. The king-size bed was empty. London was gone.

Chapter 21

"What do you mean, missing?" Ike Sr. bellowed.

"Probably not missing," Ace amended, hating his poor choice of words. "I just can't find her."

"Do you normally call the police if a model can't be found?" Ike's question dripped sarcasm and disbelief.

At 9:00 p.m., an hour past the time London and Ace were to meet her parents at the city's famed Michelin-starred restaurant, Il Luogo di Aimo e Nadia, they now stood with a frantic Ace, worried Tyler, frazzled Mira and two Italian police officers in the hotel lobby. After waiting half an hour for her to arrive and their calls going to voice mail, London's parents had called OTB, who'd tracked down Ace. When he was finally forced to tell them the truth, that he didn't know London's whereabouts, they'd come over immediately.

"You say you last saw her a couple hours ago?" A serious question that, delivered in a heavy Italian accent, sounded like a song.

"Around four," Ace replied through gritted teeth.

"And she was wearing a sundress and sandals? Did you see those clothes in her room?"

"I didn't look for her clothes," Ace yelled in frustration. "I'm looking for her!"

"Please." The other officer, a slight, pleasant-looking man with a shock of black hair and kind brown eyes, stepped toward Ace. "I understand that this form of questioning must be incredibly nerve-racking. But it's necessary to give us what we need. Often, when people are upset and not thinking clearly, wrong answers are given. That's why questions are sometimes repeated. It gives the person time to calm down a bit and think more clearly."

Ace nodded and took a calming breath that was not so calming.

"Now, did she say anything that would give a clue as to where she might go? Does she know anyone here that she'd perhaps go visit? Or the mall? It's close by and—"

"We've checked there already. I sent a team over and they scoured every inch of it, showed her picture to employees in every open store. No one had seen her. I've personally circled this area a half dozen times, called her phone so many times that it now goes straight to voice mail."

Mr. No-Nonsense Police Officer scowled. "I still don't understand why you called us. You say she's a smart, capable world traveler who's been gone for a few hours. There are a dozen perfectly logical explanations for where she could be. Unless there's something else you can share with us to prove otherwise, I see no sign of danger or reason for us to stick around."

Ace ran a frustrated hand through shiny coils as tight as his stomach was right now. London had blown off the gifts as the innocent attention of a superfan. Ace felt differently. He was sure she wouldn't want her parents to know what had been going on. But he had to tell them, had to let the detectives know about earlier today.

"Actually, there is. She's been getting—"

"Clarisse!" Jennifer pushed past Ace and ran toward her daughter. Ace and Ike Sr. were close behind.

"London!"

"Daughter, are you all right?"

London wobbled toward them—heels in hand, clothes askew—but seemingly okay.

"Baby, are you okay? Can you walk?"

London nodded, then grabbed her head. "Ow!"

"We need to call a doctor." Jennifer's strained voice conveyed her worry.

"No, Mom. I'm fine. Just need to lie down."

Ace, London, her parents and the police officers all walked toward the stairs—there was no elevator in the quaint hotel.

Once they reached them, Ace swooped her up.

"Ace, I can walk."

"I don't care."

The concerned hotel manager followed behind them. "Excuse me. Is everything all right here? Is there anything I can do, anything that you need?"

"Yes," Jennifer replied. "Please have a pot of tea sent to her room. And call a doctor!"

"Mom, no!"

Ike Sr. interrupted, "Don't argue with your mother."

They reached the suite. Ace looked at Ike Sr. "The key card is in my back pocket."

Ike Sr. pulled it out and unlocked the door then stepped back so Ace could enter. He walked straight to the bedroom and laid London on the bed. Jennifer walked to the other side and crawled over to her daughter, fluffed up two pillows behind London's head and felt her forehead for a fever.

"Sweetheart, what happened?" She continued to brush damp tendrils away from her daughter's face.

"I…I don't know."

The no-nonsense police officer stepped forward. "Ma'am, what is the last thing you remember?"

London closed her eyes and began lifting herself up. Ace and Jennifer helped her to a sitting position. Her creased brow showed the effort it took to answer that simple question.

"Carly came in. I couldn't find my…makeup-removing cream and called her to ask about it. She found it for me. And then…water. I asked her to bring me a bottle of water from the kitchen. That's the last thing."

The nice officer stood at the foot of the bed. "Where is that water bottle, Miss—what is her name?"

"London," Ace answered.

"Clarisse," Ike and Jennifer said in harmony.

"Miss London Clarisse," Nice Officer continued, "where is the bottle of water you drank?"

"It was there." London pointed toward the nightstand that was bare except for a lamp. "I'm remembering more clearly now. I drank some of it as I took off my makeup. About half. Then I came in here to take off my clothes and…" She looked down and saw the same sundress she'd worn on the plane. "I felt so tired I just laid down. But I don't remember getting up. And I definitely don't remember going to where the driver said he picked me up."

"Driver?" Ike asked. "What driver, Clarisse?"

"The car that dropped me off just now. I woke up and was in this man's car. I freaked out so much he had to pull over."

"Who is this man?" Jennifer asked.

"I don't know! He calmed me down, told me someone had told him to pick me up."

Ace sat on the bed, reached for her hand. "From where, babe?"

"The Palazzo Primo."

"Why would you be there, honey?"

"It's where our show is happening." Ace looked at No-Nonsense Officer. "Do you have probable cause to move forward now?"

Room service arrived with a cart bearing tea, water, sandwiches and soup. The manager had returned as well and was questioned by the officers as they took a full report. A detective was called in. He talked to everyone in the room along with the doorman and front desk clerk. Carly was questioned. For all, the answer was the same. *"Non lo so. Non ho visto niente."* No one knew anything. No one saw anything. Carly had taken the incident personally, breaking down in tears.

"It's not your fault," Ace told her.

"But I feel like it is. What if there was something in the water? I gave it to her."

"And you're sure the seal wasn't broken?"

"Yes. I unscrewed the cap and it was definitely sealed."

All contents of the refrigerator and minibar were removed for analysis. The room was dusted for prints. A doctor arrived and examined London. Blood was taken for analysis. Finally, two hours later, London had been moved from her suite into a two-bedroom suite at her parents' hotel. An OTB team assistant had been sent to retrieve her things. While Ace talked to Ike about recent events, Jennifer got London showered and tucked into bed.

Two somber faces greeted her when she walked into the living room.

"How is she?" both Ike Sr. and Ace asked.

"Already asleep." Jennifer sat on the couch next to Ike. He placed a comforting arm around her.

"Clarisse is in trouble, honey," Ike Sr. said. "Ace tells me she's received anonymous packages, starting at Papa Dee's home going in Temecula."

"Oh, no! Why didn't she tell us?"

"She thought it was just another overzealous fan," Ace explained. "At first I did, too. Wouldn't be the first time."

"How'd they know her schedule, where she stayed?"

"Most likely the internet, Mrs. Drake. If you search hard enough and long enough, you can find out anything."

Ike didn't have any questions. "We're taking her home."

"No. I'm staying."

Three pairs of eyes turned to see a tousled London walking toward them.

"Honey, what are you doing up?"

"Preventing you from planning my future, from the sounds of it."

"Clarisse, honey, this is too serious to ignore. We are not going to allow you to remain where it's unsafe."

London fell into a side chair. "Please, guys. Mom, Dad, I know you're concerned. I understand. But I've got a job to do, and I'm not going to run away." She fixed her parents with a determined stare. "Drakes don't run."

It took an hour, but London and Ace teamed up to convince her parents that every precaution would be taken to make sure nothing else happened. Another hour before they agreed to continue seeing all of Italy as previously planned. They attended the show. No one watching would have guessed the ordeal London had experienced the night before. She was flawless. Electric. *Bravissima! Sei unica!* These words dominated the next day's headlines as the hailed her as beautiful, unique, a woman on top.

Early the next morning, London invited Ace to lunch with her parents before they left Milan.

"I'm counting on you to protect my daughter," Ike Sr. said as the two men shook hands. "If anything happens to her, you'll answer to me."

"I understand, sir." Ace confidently returned Ike Sr.'s firm handshake. "I'll deliver her home safely. You have my word."

As he watched London's parents walk away, Ace would have been lying to say he wasn't extremely concerned about making sure that London stayed safe. But he did know one thing—he was the man for the job.

Chapter 22

One more show. By the time they arrived in Paris, this phrase was London's mantra. She'd done hundreds of fashion shows. Had logged thousands of flight hours, crossed several time zones in one day. But the added responsibility as the face of the line, a de facto spokesperson, was another beast altogether.

With every show, requests for guest appearances and interviews doubled, then tripled. Two company-hired photographers followed her constantly. Oh, and there was that little incident of being taken from a hotel, dropped into a black hole for hours and awakened by a stranger driving her back to a hotel she'd not remembered leaving. Like any trouper would, she assured everyone that she was fine. That was 70 percent true. The other 30 percent was groggy, paranoid and scared out of her mind. What happened in those hours she couldn't remember? Where'd she go? How'd she get there? Who had taken her? Why?

The detectives wanted answers to these questions. But not more than she did.

The day after the show in Milan, Ace had insisted she take the day off. She had, and aside from too many questions about the packages, they'd had an enjoyable visit. In fact, her father hadn't stopped asking questions until she refused to answer another one. Talk about overprotective. But after being in Ace's "care" for the past twenty-four hours, she was sure he'd invented the word. Tyler and Lucien had taken over all preparations for the Paris show. Guest appearances were set up at the house—no, fortress—OTB had rented. No more hotels, doormen or concierges. Ace became all of them. He had a new title. Bodyguard.

"London, what are you doing?"

"Oh, my God, Ace. I'm using the bathroom, what do you think?"

"Why do you have the door locked?"

London's face showed the incredulity she felt. "Seriously?"

Did that door handle actually just rattle? Yes. It did.

"Leave me alone, Ace. You're like a warden trying to arrest an inmate already in jail."

"Ha! I'm here for a reason. Your last taping is in an hour. *Entertainment International.* They're a big deal. We're setting up in the parlor. Hair and makeup are already down there. The stylist is readying your wardrobe." He rattled the knob again. "Don't be late."

London shook her head and began to chuckle. His antics were so ridiculous she couldn't even be mad.

Her phone rang. She exited the bathroom and rushed to catch it. If it was her parents and she didn't answer, they'd be on the next plane.

"Hello? Hey, Max, hold on. You can go on down, Carly. I'll meet you down there."

"Someone is supposed be with you at all times, London. Ace's orders."

"I'll handle Ace. Go on down." London walked with Carly to the bedroom door and closed it behind her. She hit the speaker button and fell back on the bed. "Jeez!"

"London? Everything all right?"

"Everything would be fine if I stopped getting asked if I'm all right."

"Calm down, darling. You sound exasperated. That's the only reason I asked. You know I care about you."

"I know. It's just been crazy over here."

"Sounds like I arrived just in time."

"You're in Paris?"

"*Oui, oui.* And wanting to take you out tonight if you have time."

London had all but been in prison since the Milan incident. If a hair on her head moved, Ace knew which direction. An evening with the laid-back lover turned friend now sounded like heaven.

"I'm getting ready to tape a TV segment. I'll have to see what's up after that. Call you later?"

"I'll be waiting."

She hung up the phone, called her parents and quickly scrolled through her emails. Checking the time, something she'd done more since working with Ace than she'd done in her whole career combined, she headed out the door.

He was coming down the hall. "You're late."

"Five minutes. Give me a break, Ace. You're not my dad."

"I'm damn close to it. I gave Mr. Drake my word to

take care of you, and no matter how much it gets on your nerves I'm going to do just that. Now, let's go be amazing."

She was more than that. London was an interviewer's dream: funny, smart, engaging. The show's producers had allotted two hours for the shoot. Forty-five minutes later, they packed up their gear.

Ace had been on phone calls during much of the taping but came back to the parlor once they were done.

"She was excellent," the host told him. "Having her as your spokesperson is the best move you've ever made."

"I can't disagree."

While Ace talked to the producers, London walked over to Samantha, who'd helped set up the shoot. "What's next?"

"That's it, kid. You're done for the day. Ace talked about us all going out to dinner."

London shook her head. "I've got other plans. A good friend of mine is in town, so we're going to hang out."

"Oh, okay. Have fun."

London pulled out her cell phone, tapping Max's number as she bopped up the steps.

"Hey, guess what."

"Hello there, gorgeous."

"I'm free! What are we doing?"

"What about front-row tickets to an Adele show followed by a late-night dinner party with Channe Bonfils?"

"Are you serious?"

In the fashion world, Channe Bonfils and his dinner parties were legendary. An eccentric royal with more money than God, he lived in a palace that rivaled Versailles and was rarely seen in public. London was all in.

"There's only one problem. Well, actually, two. First of all, I don't have anything here that will meet his dress code. Those parties are strictly haute couture."

"I have a few connections here. We'll get you something breathtaking. What's the second problem?"

"Ace."

"So you two are dating?"

"It's a long story."

"It's a yes-or-no story."

"Look, not now, Max."

"Fair enough. Where should we meet?"

"That's tricky."

"Because of the long story?" London huffed. "Does this have anything to do with your earlier mood? What's going on?"

"I'll tell you about it but later, okay? I don't want to get into it now. This might get a bit uncomfortable, but you're going to have to come get me. Seeing you in person is the only way Ace will let me leave."

"You're kidding me, right?"

"No, I was kidnapped. Like I said, long story. I'll tell you the details on the way to Channe. What time should I expect you?"

"Let me make a few calls, get something that will make you the belle of the ball, and then I'll call you back."

She'd showered before the taping, but London went into the bathroom and formed a quick ablution. She stood in front of the mirror naked, critiquing. Like every other woman with blood and a pulse, when looking in a mirror she highlighted imperfections. Breasts too small. Forehead too big. Torso too long and lanky. Not curvy like her cousin Katrina or her sister, Teresa. More like the giraffe she'd been teasingly called growing up. Fortunately, years of wearing top-of-the-line fashions from the world's most talented designers had taught her how to downplay her faults and highlight her assets, one being that giraffe neck that had garnered so much teasing. She piled her freshly redone extensions on the top of her head, secured them with pins and pulled down a few tendrils for just the right amount of sexy. After touching up her makeup, she walked to the closet, pulled out a simple, one-sleeved multicolored maxi and a pair of gold-and-silver mesh boots. Almost two dozen bangles covered her arm. She pulled on a pair of dangling two-toned earrings and kept her neck bare. No matter what color, the mixture of metals would complement the gown. A spritz of perfume and London was ready to go. She stood back from the full-length mirror and surveyed her handiwork.

"Where are you going?"

London turned to Ace. "I didn't hear a knock."

"The door was open. Samantha thinks you're not joining us for dinner. Where are you going?"

London bit back a caustic response and decided on a more sensible route. "Max is in town. He's invited me to a dinner party."

"London, you know I can't let you go to that."

The statement pushed sensible out of the room. "Let me go? Did I really just hear that? You can't *let* me go? Who do you think you are, Ace Montgomery?"

"The man who promised your father he'd protect you."

"The problem with that conversation that happened between you and my father is that I wasn't in it. I don't need your protection, okay? I can take care of myself."

"Oh, yeah? Like you did in Milan?"

Bam. That jab pierced the cocky protective armor and nipped her heart.

"Forget you, Ace." She reached for her jeweled clutch and tried to sweep past him.

He grabbed her arm. "You're actually going to walk out that door and defy me? Aren't you even a little concerned for your life?"

London looked from Ace's eyes to his fingers clutching her bare arm. Her stilettos allowed her to look him dead in his eye. With the daggers shot from her livid glance, it's a wonder Ace didn't go blind. Her tone, low and deadly, was pushed through gritted teeth. "Get. Your. Hands. Off. Me."

Ace dropped it immediately. "I'm sorry, London. I didn't mean to grab you like that. The reaction came out of how worried I am about your safety, about how much I care."

"Ace." London sighed. "What happened happened. What could have been worse wasn't. Either way, it's in the past. I can't do anything about that or about what might take place tomorrow. I can only control what happens right now. And I'm not going to stop living my life just because some wacko is spending too much time focusing on me while living his.

"Besides, Max knows everything that's been going on. He's just as concerned about my safety as you are."

Ace snorted. "I just bet he is."

"What's that supposed to mean?"

"You know exactly what it means. Max isn't concerned about your safety. He's concerned about his ego and appearances and feeling bad that he got dumped. But you're too much like him to see you're being played."

"Oh, is that so?" She took another step.

"Damn right it is." They stood nose to nose.

London pushed him away. "And who are you? The knight in shining armor trying to rescue the damsel and stroke your massive ego to a size bigger than it already is? Supposedly so concerned about my safety? I'll tell you what you're concerned about. Your precious company. OTB's reputation. Your name. Your brand. At the end of the day, that's what you're really protecting. So don't come at me with that self-righteous attitude, like you have a lock on what I'm all about. You think you can stand there and dictate to me because of a promise? Because you think you know me? Think again."

If Ace had given any thought to backing down, it was short-lived.

"I may not know everything. But I'll tell you what I do know. I know you're a spoiled, selfish brat who grew up in the lap of luxury and ate baby food from a silver spoon. I know you are a fabulous model who's let success go to your head and jade you into someone who can't see that on her worst day she lives better than ninety-nine percent of the world's population on their best. Who has wanted for nothing, hasn't ever struggled or had to overcome a challenge in a day of her pampered life!"

"I've had to overcome plenty!" London raged, argue mode full-blown.

"What? Name one thing." Ace was just as angry. Their voices grew louder with each retort.

"I don't have to answer to you!"

"No, you can't answer because you don't have an answer!"

"You don't know what I have or what I've gone through."

"Yes, I do. You've gone through nothing! Even survived a kidnapping without so much as a scratch!"

London's voice now shook with anger. "Don't think everybody who smells good and looks nice has lived perfect, trouble-free lives. I've gone through things, okay?"

"Like what?"

London stepped to him, lowered her voice to a whisper, her eyes shining. "Like being violated, physically, against my will. Don't be so quick to judge, Ace. Some people carry scars the world can't see."

London's cell phone pinged. She snatched it up along with her clutch and ran out the door.

"London! Wait!"

But she didn't. She ran from Ace, and her past, to a dinner party where laughter and loud music would make her forget. Just as they always had.

Chapter 23

Ace felt worse than horrible. He felt numb. Just after midnight London had sent a text. I'm safe, it began. Typed with sarcasm, Ace imagined. Followed by the news that she wouldn't be returning to the house. That she'd meet them at the venue. He'd gone to bed then. But unable to sleep, he'd spent the night tossing and turning.

London's parting words echoed on a loop in his head. No, not London. It was Clarisse who'd spoke the truth last night. Who'd looked at him with quivering lips, whose eyes had watered with vulnerability and unresolved pain. *Don't think everybody who smells good and looks nice has lived perfect, trouble-free lives...lives...lives. I've gone through things, okay? Like being violated... violated...violated. Don't be so quick to judge...judge... judge. Some people carry scars the world can't see. The world can't see. The world can't see.*

He'd instructed Frida to let him know the moment

London arrived. He found her in hair and makeup. "Can I have a word with you?"

"Sure. What's up?"

The armor was on. The guard was up. London had returned.

"In private, please. Just a couple minutes."

"Okay, but that's all I've got."

She got up from the chair and followed Ace into the hallway. She stood there, arms crossed, looking away.

"About last night… I'm sorry."

"No worries."

"Please, I understand the tough-girl thing."

London gave him the side eye.

His hands raised in defense. "Okay, *appreciate* would be a better way to say it. I appreciate you being defensive. After how I acted last night, you have every right. I was way out of line. Judging, like you said. Inserting myself where I didn't belong. I didn't know…"

He watched her jaw ripple as she clenched and unclenched it. "Nobody does."

"Nobody? Not even your family?"

"I don't want to talk about it. We've got a show to do. I need to get ready."

Over. Done. She walked away.

There was a saying in entertainment—the show must go on. It did. And again, London was everything. Like life was perfect. Like she didn't have a care in the world. After a finale that garnered a two-minute standing ovation, she walked off the stage, changed clothes and left the building. London was done with Europe. Ace left the country believing she might also be done with OTB. Her…and him.

Back home, OTB remained closed for the rest of the week, to give those who'd managed the four-week fashion jaunt some well-deserved time off. Ace spent time with his parents, Christine and Hank, and was happy when an old college buddy invited him to Vegas for a weekend with the boys. Gave him a chance to escape his thoughts and not think about the unreturned phone calls he'd placed to London. And what that meant. She ignored him, yet he was reminded of her every waking moment. Ads, the OTB website, catalogs and press. As if that wasn't enough, she'd invaded his dreams, as well. Turned them into nightmares. Last night he'd dreamed someone had snatched her backstage at a fashion show. He woke up trying to sprint with legs entangled in sheets.

Monday finally arrived and along with it the fashion-week wrap-up, a recap and brainstorming meeting held twice a year. As much as he wanted to get back to work, he wasn't necessarily thrilled about this meeting and what he had to share with the team. But after wading through a slew of emails, returning a couple urgent phone calls and plotting out the week's to-do list, Ace walked into the company break room for a fortifying cup of joe. Tyler was there already, eating empty calories covered in glaze.

"Morning, Ace! How's it going?"

"Time will tell."

"That bad, huh?" Tyler finished his doughnut, licked his fingers and reached for another. "You talk to London?"

"Nope. Left messages. So far she hasn't returned my calls." Ace poured cream into a cup of hazelnut-flavored coffee. "It's all good."

Tyler studied him over the coffee cup's rim. "If you say so. What about your time off? Do anything exciting?"

"I've had enough excitement over the past four weeks to last a lifetime. I chilled, mostly. Spent time with the folks. Met some friends in Las Vegas. What about you?"

"Tahiti, baby, and let me tell you—those folk know how to relax. Phillip fell in love with the island, threatened to relocate."

Mira walked by the break room, doubled back and stuck her head in the door. "I was headed to the conference room. Is the meeting still happening there or should I come in here and pull up a chair?"

"Good morning to you, too, Mira," Ace replied.

"Come on, boys. Vacation's over. The quicker we get this day over, the faster the week will go."

They followed her to the conference room and settled around the table. Though the three were equal partners, Ace was the unofficial head of the team, reflected in how both Tyler and Mira waited for him to begin.

"First of all, I want to thank you guys for stepping up, going over and above to make sure this launch was successful. It went way beyond that. I don't think any of us expected to get the exposure, press, accolades and everything that's happened in the past four weeks. I just started wading through emails and one after another presents offers for advertising and articles—I even saw one with a reality-show proposal attached."

"Not a chance," Tyler said with a groan.

"Not so fast," Mira countered. "For all of their antics, reality television is a multibillion-dollar industry, and the fastest-growing genre on TV." Mira drank from her bottle of water. "I actually think we should entertain the idea. London has an interest in expanding into television. She has that Kardashian quality—people want a peek into her life. I think she'd be perfect."

Ace shifted in his seat. "Speaking of London, I guess I need to share a little more about what happened in France. I didn't want to talk about it on the plane ride home, partly because I'd hoped that by now it would have sorted itself out. But it hasn't, and since my personal actions might impact the business, you guys need to be aware.

"Back in Milan, London's father personally tasked me with ensuring her safety for the duration of the European tour. I tried to do that, with the best of intentions. But London's willfulness is well-known. I don't know how I forgot. But I did. London wasn't on the plane with us because we had a huge fight."

"What about?"

"The reason isn't important right now. I bring it up for two reasons. One, because as of now London may or may not want to continue as the face of Her. And two, for us, that might be a good thing."

Tyler's feigned cough turned to laughter. "You're pulling our legs, right?"

"That wasn't a joke."

Mira sat back in her chair. "London was the best thing that ever could have happened for the line. The launch wouldn't have been the same without her."

"I won't disagree with that."

"I knew you were smart."

"Ace, come on man. Give us one good reason we'd spend two seconds discussing London not being the face for OTB Her."

"I'll give you several. First, for all the benefit she brings to the table—and the benefits are immense—she also comes with liabilities. The crazed stalker or crazed fan or whoever is sending gifts all over the world. The kidnapping attempt. Not only are we putting her in danger with this added exposure, but we're setting ourselves up for possible harm, as well.

"What happened in Milan was terrifying and could have yielded a much more tragic result. I care for London, and had something happened to her while doing business for us, we all would have been personally devastated. But had something happened and her family held us responsible somehow, such a move could be catastrophic to the company, as well. The OTB Her line could go down as fast as it went up. The men's line and every idea we have in the pipeline would be affected."

"You're throwing out a lot of supposition here, Ace."

"Mira, I—"

"Please, Ace, give me a second before you go on. I don't know where all of this is coming from, but it's not from the Ace I know. The man I quit my corporate job for and reached into my retirement fund to get into partnership with wouldn't be focusing on doom-and-gloom what-ifs. Life happens. The show's over. We have a few months before the spring shows, to either find out who's after her or devise a way to make sure he doesn't get her on our watch. But anyone else being the Her girl? For me, that's out of the question."

"I have to agree with Mira, Ace. When it comes to anyone else repping this line, London has no competition or comparison. As Phillip would say, she shut it down."

"The publicist's phone hasn't stopped ringing," Mira continued. "The sales department is being deluged. We've gotten orders from all the majors, Neiman, Saks, Bloomingdale's, all placing big orders and making room on their floors for a full OTB Her display. Yes, it's partly because of the clothes. The designs are amazing. But for the women buying those clothes, it's not just about style. It's about feeling a little like the fabulous, fearless, take-charge, screw-the-world woman they see promoting the looks. It's about putting a little London into their lives."

"I don't disagree with any of that, Mira. And I'm still that man for whom you took a risk. It's not about touting doom and gloom, it's about looking at every aspect of business objectively, from all angles. Discussing it. Debating it. And coming to a mutual conclusion.

"On Friday, I called the detective in Milan. They still have no suspects and no solid lead on either the package or the attempted kidnapping. The mail we sent back went to a virtual mail store and a randomly chosen address that didn't have a corresponding box to the number listed."

"What about the rape kit?"

"That was the one piece of good news. There was no evidence that's she'd been assaulted—sexually or otherwise.

"To give a partial answer to your earlier question, Tyler, and to comment on what Mira said about keeping London safe, our argument in Paris began about that very thing. When she went against me and my word to her father and left the house, she left my protection and care. If something had happened to her it wouldn't have been about her being a grown woman or highly traveled or any of that. It would have been that I'd given my word and didn't follow through. We all know how she can be. The same temperamental, stubborn, rebel qualities that make her great are also what can make it very difficult for us to keep her out of danger. Like you said, whoever did this is still out there. As a company, do we want to take the risk?"

Ace had purposely kept the focus on the company and what he'd promised Ike Sr. but his fear of harm coming to London went much deeper, straight through his heart.

Tyler folded his arms and eyed Ace intently. "Tell me something, Ace. Is this just about London's safety, or does it also have to do with the person you demanded I ban from the shows, the one who showed up in Paris, whose face along with hers is splashed all over the tabloids with them all lovey-dovey at some kind of suave affair?"

"I don't know what you're talking about."

"I think you do."

"This isn't personal. It's business."

Ace said this, and another recording began to play in his head. *I'll tell you what you're concerned about. Your precious company. OTB's reputation. Your name. Your brand. At the end of the day, that's what you're really protecting.*

"Guys, here's my suggestion. I say we contact London or her agent and make sure she's still on board. Remind them of the contract she signed. Because if she isn't, we've already wasted an hour discussing someone who's no longer with the company." Mira looked at Ace. "Do you want me to handle this?"

"No. I'll handle it."

Later that day, Ace set about doing just that. Another call to London went to voice mail, but that didn't stop him. He went home and changed into comfortable clothes. Grabbed a meal at a drive-through, programmed his GPS and steered his top-of-the-line Porsche in the direction of Paradise Cove.

Chapter 24

It was quiet. A sound London hated. It was one of the reasons she worked so hard, traveled so much, stayed so busy. Distracting relationships and a raucous lifestyle drowned out memories mostly dead and buried. Whispery images that every now and then would try and creep into her consciousness, begging to be resolved. Drakes didn't run, but for more than ten years she'd beaten a steady trot away from a series of incidents she'd never before shared. Until last week. When Ace pushed a button hard enough to open her up.

"I can't deal with this boring town. Coming home was a big mistake."

She grabbed her purse, keys and shades and headed for the door. Once in the car, she rang Quinn.

"What are you doing?"

"Hey, London. I'm visiting my grandmother. What about you?"

"Bored out of my mind. Want to get together and, I don't know, do whatever you guys do in this place?"

Quinn's laughter, usually contagious, grated on her nerves. "You sound so much like me when I first got here. I didn't think I'd last a week, let alone the six months I'd promised Grand. You'll get used to it, maybe even learn to enjoy it as I do now. Something about the slower pace allows you to reconnect with yourself, hear yourself think, you know?"

"More than you realize."

"Grand and I were just about to have dinner. Would you like to join us?"

"Sounds good, but no. I'm having big-city withdrawal and need a little excitement."

"What time is it, seven o'clock? Right now you have the choice between bingo at city hall, skating at the community center or watching the ripples at Drake Lake."

"Very funny, Quinn."

"Why don't you do what you really want to do and return Ace's calls? I don't know what you argued about, but nothing's so bad that it can be fixed."

"There's no fixing necessary where that's concerned. Ace and I were just having fun, doing what some models do when stuck on a tour together. That situation was more about business than anything."

"Was? Aren't you forgetting you're the face of the line?"

"Yeah, well, I don't know if that's what I want to be anymore."

"London, what's really going on?"

London pulled into a strip mall. Located on the main road that went through the town, it was a place where teenagers often came to meet their friends, drink beer smuggled from their parents' homes and to see and be seen by all passing by. London watched a group of girls laughing and joking with a boy who looked like the town jock. Happy. Carefree. Funny, until now London would have used those words to describe herself. They came close to describing her personality, but not exactly.

"London?"

"Oh, sorry, Quinn. I got distracted."

"Where are you?"

"Over by the mall. Thinking about going into Acquired Taste, having a glass of wine."

"Oh, I hate for you to drink alone. What are your brothers up to? Or your sisters-in-law. Call one of them, London. You know too many people in this town to hang out by yourself."

"You're right. Maybe I'll go over to the center, see if Terrell's still there. He's usually there late, especially if Aliyah has to work."

"Jennifer told me about the charity fashion event. She's really excited."

The fashion show. Yet another topic to remind her of Ace and how quickly he'd become entwined in her life.

"Hey, London. Dinner's ready. You sure you don't want to come over?"

"No, but thanks for the offer. Give Grand a hug for me."

"Will do."

London ended the call. Head in hand, she muttered out loud, "London, what are you doing?"

A commotion began among the teens nearby.

"Whoa!"

"Hey, y'all, that's my car!"

"Man, you wish you could drive something like that."

"What is that?" one girl asked.

"Looks like a Firebird," another answered.

High School Jock pushed the girl who'd answered. "Y'all don't know nothing. That's a Porsche."

Porsche? London lifted her head. The light turned green. A shiny silver Porsche, driven by a man bearing a striking resemblance to Ace Montgomery, drove directly past her.

Was that…? No. Couldn't be. Not here in Paradise Cove, California.

She slammed her car into gear. "Okay, girl, you really need to get it together." Zooming out of the parking lot, she headed to Drake Community Center, where her charismatic brother Terrell could keep her entertained, or at least provide enough conversation to keep her mind off…everything. Turning up the car stereo, she tried to put yet another layer between her and her thoughts.

A call coming through her car's Bluetooth interrupted the music.

"Hey, Mom."

"Hello, Clarisse. Where are you, sweetie?"

"On my way to the center."

"Well, you need to turn around and come home. You have a visitor."

"Who?"

Asked even though she already knew the answer.

"I'll let it be a lovely surprise. Just come home quickly. You passed on dinner, but we can all share dessert."

Less than ten minutes later, she walked into the house and down the hall toward Jennifer's tinkling laughter, Ike Sr.'s rumbling chuckle and the deep, slightly raspy sound of Ace's voice. Great. Just friggin' great.

Go ahead. Impress them. I couldn't care less about that or you.

She took a quick glance in a hallway mirror, pulled

the band off a hastily arranged ponytail and shook out her hair.

When she turned the corner, her greeting was abrupt. "What are you doing here?"

"Clarisse!" Jennifer's cultured sensibilities chafed at her rudeness.

If Ace was ruffled, it didn't show. "Hello, London."

"Hello. What are you doing here?"

"I wanted to speak with you, but you haven't returned my calls."

"Which should have been your clue."

"Can we talk privately?"

London glared at him for a few seconds, then turned and walked out of the room.

Ace stood quickly, addressing London's parents just as fast. "Mr. and Mrs. Drake, it's been a pleasure. Excuse me. London!"

His long legs ate up the distance between them, catching her as she headed—more like stomped—up the stairs. She reached the top and spun around. "You've got a lot of nerve coming here."

"Yes, I do."

She continued down the hall. "A lot of good it did. Because I have nothing to say to you."

"Good. It'll make listening easier."

"You're such a jerk."

"That's not my intention."

They reached her suite. She flung open the door and whirled around on him. "Okay, talk. Your five minutes start now."

Ace eyed her intently for a moment.

"Staring at me is just wasting time."

Another beat and then he said, "I love you."

Well, now. This was an unexpected opening line, one

that shocked London into silence. From the look on Ace's face, she suspected it might have shocked him, too.

"Bad timing, I know. But I can't help it, can't control it. I tried to. Wouldn't even admit it to myself until tonight when I had a two hour drive to think about why not hearing from you, being with you, was driving me crazy. But I've known for a while. In London, I knew. And Milan. I especially knew in Paris, when you stayed out with Max and I couldn't sleep. When I wanted nothing more than to crash that dinner party and introduce my fist to his face. Me, a nonviolent kind of brother.

"Earlier, I told myself this was about business. That the only reason I was coming here was to confirm your continued participation as the face of our line. But that was bullshit. I'm here because I didn't want to be without you for one second longer. Is there a way you can forgive me so we can at least be friends?"

London continued to stare at him, still stuck back on that I-love-you moment. Slowly, she began to nod her head. "I guess," she whispered and walked into his embrace.

His hug was long and firm, his hands squeezing her shoulders and back. He kissed her forehead, cheeks and eyes. Then he stepped back and away from her.

"I'm so sorry I hurt you. I felt so bad about all I said, especially when you told me you'd been molested."

"I wish I hadn't said that. Like I said then, I've never told anyone."

"Why not?"

"Too hard to talk about. Easier to forget."

"Maybe you should talk about it."

"Yes, Clarisse, maybe you should."

London gasped. Ace slowly turned around. Jennifer stood in the doorway, her expression horrified.

Chapter 25

"Mom!"

"Is that true, Clarisse? Have you been molested?"

"Why were you eavesdropping?"

"Honey, I wasn't. The intercom went out. I came up because Junior called and invited us to join them at the club. I hoped you two would join us. But I can't ignore what I overheard." She turned to Ace. "Would you mind giving us some privacy?"

"No, ma'am. Not at all."

"You can rejoin Ike downstairs if you'd like. He's either in his office or the library. At the bottom of the stairs, make a left and head down that center hall."

"I'll find it."

He reached out and gave London's arm a gentle squeeze. "It'll be okay, London."

Jennifer crossed over to a love seat, sat and patted the space beside her. "Come sit down, honey."

"Mom, I really don't want to do this."

"I know you don't. My heart is breaking that you even have to, because it means that something tragic happened to my darling baby girl on my watch and I didn't even know."

London walked over and sat next to her mother. She took Jennifer's hands. "Don't blame yourself, Mommy. It wasn't on your watch. By the time I saw you, I'd already buried the pain. There's no way you could have known."

"Please, sweetheart. Tell me what happened. Who did this to you? When?"

London slowly rose and began pacing the room. When she spoke, her back was to Jennifer as she gazed out the window.

"It was in New Orleans. During the time all of us kids would be down at Grandpa Walter's farm. One day I was wandering around the property and heard a sound in the barn, like a baby crying. I was curious and went inside. It was dark and I'd just come out of bright sunlight, so I couldn't really see. Once my eyes adjusted I saw one of the farmhands, Mr. Williams, standing over by a stall. I was frightened, didn't know anyone was in there. But he smiled and beckoned me over. Said a horse had just had her foal and asked if I wanted to see it."

She turned then, leaned against the window ledge and stared into her history. "You know me, I was never much of a farm girl. Had never seen a baby horse. But I liked Mr. Williams, so strong and handsome. He was always so polite to Grandpa and nice to me. I didn't hesitate. I went over, saw this beautiful little replica of the horse beside it. He told me to touch it, but I was scared. He said, 'Rub her coat, just like this.' And he rubbed a finger up and down my arm. It made me feel funny, uncomfortable. A tingling in places I'd never before experienced. I backed away, told him I didn't want to touch the horse. That I wanted to go back outside. He told me I couldn't. Not until I…did certain things."

"Did he rape you, honey?"

London looked at her mother. Watched tears, one after the other, run down her face and off her chin.

She shook her head. "Not…exactly. He touched me and made me touch him. He warned me to not tell anyone. Said that no one would believe me, a kid, that I'd get in a whole lot of trouble. That I'd shame Grandpa Walter, Grandma Claire and the family. Then he used those words as blackmail to get me back in the barn almost every day for a week, until vacation was over and we finally came back home."

"Clarisse, baby, why didn't you tell me?"

"Didn't you hear what I just said? I couldn't!" London returned to the love seat. The two women faced each other. "Drake pride has been instilled in me from the time I was born. All of my brothers and Teresa, they lived up to the high expectations. I was trying to do the same and knew it couldn't happen if my secret was exposed. I couldn't bear shaming my family. I knew you'd be so disappointed and ashamed."

"But it wasn't your fault."

"I know that now. I didn't at twelve years old."

Jennifer pondered all that had been said, her eyes narrowing as she too stared into the past. "Now it all makes sense. That's around the time you started acting out, so much so that…"

"You sent me off to boarding school."

"You did that on purpose."

"It wasn't planned. But after it happened, I felt the one good thing to come out of it was no more summers in New Orleans. No more chance of seeing Mr. Williams."

Jennifer gathered London into her arms. Began to slowly rock them. "Clarisse Alana, my dear, feisty, beautiful darling. I'm sorry. So, so sorry that you've carried this burden alone for all of these years."

They held each other for a long, tender moment. When she pulled back, London's eyes glistened with tears. "Don't tell anybody, okay, Mom? I don't want anyone else to know."

"I don't think that's a promise I can make, Clarisse. I'm not sure it would be in your best interest even if I could."

"Why not? Why does anyone else have to know?"

Jennifer sighed. "Your father and I have no secrets between us. I need to know whether or not this Williams guy is still at the farm. If so, he will be dealt with immediately. But even more than that, sweetheart, it's my desire to see you totally free. As long as you feel shame for something that was not your fault, you will be in an emotional prison. It's why assaults like this continue, because victims are too ashamed and embarrassed to speak up."

A pause and then she continued, "There are others in this family who've experienced your same fate."

"Who?"

"I'll leave them to share their stories. Right now my focus is you. And I want you to know that in this moment I couldn't be prouder of the woman you are, that you are my daughter and that you bear the Drake name."

The conversation ended shortly after that. Jennifer agreed to give London a few days before sharing the news she'd just learned with the family. Back downstairs London and Ace passed on the invite to join the family at the club. Instead, he accepted their offer to spend the night in one of several guesthouses they owned around town and meet Jennifer for lunch the following day to discuss the charity show.

London rode with Ace and directed him to his temporary abode. They pulled into the driveway of a two-story beach-style house with flowering shrubbery and a well-manicured yard. "This is it?"

"Yep."

He shut off the engine. "Y'all call this a guesthouse? You guys sure know how to treat your guests."

"Makes it easier when you own a realty company with architecture and construction arms. Come on. Let's go inside."

Ace continued to be impressed. London gave a five-minute tour that ended in the kitchen. After pouring drinks, they settled into the living room.

"Still mad at me?"

London shook her head. "It's crazy. All these years I've held on to that secret, feeling horrible about what happened and scared someone would find out. But Mom was amazing. She made me feel…" Tears formed in her eyes. "Her words were like healing waters. They made me feel clean again."

"Oh, baby." Ace put down his drink and pulled London into his arms. He pulled away far enough to brush tendrils of hair away from her face. "You are amazing. Don't ever doubt that."

"Oh, yeah? I thought I was a spoiled, pampered brat."

"A little of that, too. But mostly amazing." A companionable silence filled the room. London relaxed into the embrace, still bewildered that he was in her town and she was in his arms.

"The team's been worried about you. When you didn't fly back with us, there was all sorts of speculation. I wasn't in the mood to answer their questions."

"Your personal life is none of their business."

"True, but their main focus was OTB Her and whether you're still going to represent it."

"Do you still want me to?"

"Yes. You're the perfect person for the line."

"Then there's something you need to know. Pics were taken of Max and me when we were in Paris. The buzz is that we're dating again."

"I know."

"You do?"

"Mira saw the pictures and mentioned it today in the fashion week recap. It's not true, right?"

"Well…"

She felt him stiffen. He sat up and placed her away from him. "Are you back with him, London?"

"We didn't sleep together but he's wanted me back this whole time, and after our fight I told him I'd think about it."

"Where's your phone?"

"Where's my… What?"

"Your cell phone. Where is it?"

"In my purse. Why?"

"Because he needs to know that there's been a change in plans. If he wants you, he'll have to come through me. And I'm not moving."

Chapter 26

The next day, London and Ace joined her parents, Ike Jr. and Quinn, Niko and Terrell for lunch at the Paradise Cove Country Club. They were in one of the private rooms, being catered to by a personal chef.

"So, Mr. Montgomery..." Terrell's voice was cordial, his smile pleasant. "Tell us a little something about yourself."

"Don't let the smile fool you," London warned. "That question lands you squarely in the Drake hot seat."

"I like heat," Ace calmly replied. "Niko, right? Pass me those rolls, brother."

"Confident." Jennifer beamed. "I like that."

"Confident or cocky?" Ike Jr. asked, brow raised.

"Your choice," Ace said.

Terrell laughed. "My man. I like you!"

London's phone vibrated. Again.

"Turn that thing off," Niko suggested. "When your man is present, he should have your full attention."

This elicited the responses Niko expected. Indignation from the women. Laughs and agreement from the men.

"On that note—" London pushed back from the table "—I'll excuse myself for just a minute. I really need to take the call."

She left the room and walked down the hallway. Max had been calling since shortly after Ace arrived yesterday. She'd lost count of how many times. Since he was going to be upset whenever it happened, she decided to take the call, end the affair that hadn't even happened and move on with Ace and their happy life.

"Hey, Max."

"Finally. I was beginning to think I'd have to come down there."

Oh, no. Not you, too. Just the thought of Ace and Max colliding in Paradise Cove made London almost pass out.

"Sorry to keep you waiting. There's a lot going on."

"I told you not to worry about packing anything. Just move back up here. I'll buy whatever you need."

"I'm not coming, Max."

"What do you mean? Are you coming next week, next month, when?"

"There's no easy way to say this, Max. I made a mistake in Paris. We're not getting back together."

"Has Ace gotten to you? What did he say? Does it have something to do with your modeling contract? Look, I know some of the best lawyers in the world. We'll get you out of it. Pay them off. Whatever we have to do."

"It's not about the contract, Max."

"Then what is it?"

"I'm in love with Ace."

She hadn't meant to tell her ex before she told her lover. It just worked out that way.

"I don't believe it. Look, come up. Just for the week-end. If you feel the same way after, I'll leave you alone."

"I'm sorry, Max. There's no changing my mind. Please don't call again."

"Okay, London, please. I'm sorry. Let's not end an-grily. You just shocked me, that's all. Your happiness. That's always been what's most important to me. As long as you're happy, I'm happy for you."

"You mean that?"

"Of course I do. Am I hurting? Sure. You're one helluva woman. That's why I'd never want to be totally disconnected from you. We're both in entertainment. Never know when our paths could cross. So can we at least be friends?"

"I don't know, Max."

"Please?"

"Okay, fine. Friends."

"Thank you, London. Be safe."

"You, too, Max. Take care of yourself."

London returned to the table, where everyone was being entertained by her brother Terrell. She was grate-ful the attention was diverted from her. Saved her from having to answer the question that for sure was on at least one person's mind.

Until later.

"Who was it?"

Minutes after they'd left the group and were heading back to the guesthouse, the question spilled from Ace's mouth as if of its own volition.

"Who was who?" As if she didn't know.

"Never mind. Not my business."

"If you knew that, why'd you ask?"

He looked at her a long moment and said, "Because I wanted to know."

London bit back a retort. She didn't want to fight with Ace. Didn't want to change the positive vibe that had come from his surprise visit. Didn't want to close herself off from someone who'd unknowingly opened a wound and begun a healing process.

"It was Max."

"I thought so. What did he want?"

London hesitated, then told him the truth. "He wanted me to come back to Los Angeles, to move back in with him."

A long pause and then he asked, "What did you say?"

"I told him no. Want to know why?"

"Only if you want to tell me."

"I told him I couldn't move back in him with him because I'm in love with you."

Ace said nothing. London didn't know how to interpret his silence, so she became quiet, too. They reached the house. She pulled into the drive but kept the car running.

He turned to her. "You coming in?"

"Do you want me to?"

"Yes."

"Are you mad at me?"

"No."

"Then why'd you get so quiet?"

He placed his hand over the one she rested on the steering wheel and gave it a squeeze.

"Sometimes you leave me at a loss for words. Turn the car off. Come inside. I want to make love to you."

Now it was London without a comeback.

None was needed. As soon as she closed the front door, Ace scooped her up and headed for the stairs. He entered the master suite, laid her on the bed and stepped back.

His eyes swept her body. The desire she saw made her weak and shy. He removed her sandals, one at a time, and massaged her feet. His touch was light, gentle. He reached for the waistband of her wide-legged pants from the OTB fall collection, similar to the pair she tried on during that first fitting in San Francisco. They locked eyes. She lifted herself off the bed enough for him to ease the silky material over her hips and down her legs, dropping them beside him. He unbuckled, unzipped, his desire evident, outlined against the fabric. Jeans joined silky pants on the floor. Ace placed a knee on the bed. Spread her legs. Pulled aside satin and lace. Kissed her there. His tongue swirled and jabbed, teased and taunted, a heat-seeking missile aimed to please. Leisurely, lavishly he loved her. London quivered at his tender touch, writhing this way and that under his unrelenting love-making until pure ecstasy burst from her core, shattered her senses, left her sated and dazed.

There was no time to recover. In an instant Ace had removed his shirt and covered her. He positioned himself at the entry to paradise, eased inside her with a sigh. Setting up a slow and steady rhythm that could go the distance, he tapped her core with a measured intensity. Whispered sensuous intentions into her ear. Sealed his name on her soul. Changed positions and continued. London grasped the headboard to brace herself. Ace gripped her hips and moved faster, thrust deeper, sent them both tumbling into another climax before collapsing on the bed and pulling London into his arms. She cuddled against him, body still quivering, and wondered how she'd ever considered going back to Maxwell Tata. In this moment it was crystal clear that here with Ace was where she belonged.

Chapter 27

Over the next few weeks, their love declared, Ace and London juggled busy schedules to deepen their long-distance relationship. Finally it was the Memorial Day weekend. Ace had taken off work, driven down to Paradise Cove and looked forward to life with London for five straight days. He pulled into the guesthouse driveway, found the key London had left beneath a planter and went inside. A few minutes later, he heard the door open.

"Ace! Where are you?"

"Up here, baby." London bounded up the steps and into Ace's arms.

"Wow, that's some greeting. What's going on?"

"Nothing. Just happy to see you."

He pulled away to look into her eyes. "I could get used to having that kind of greeting every day."

"Hmm." London leaned in for a kiss, ending further conversation for the next several minutes.

London wore a cute minidress that gathered at the bodice and flared from the waist. Ace reached for the hem, pulled it up and palmed her satin-covered cheeks. A few seconds more and his happiness began to grow. He swirled his hips, pushed the bulge against London's waist.

"Come on. We're both wearing too many clothes."

London pulled away. "I want you so badly. But not right now. Everybody's over at Warren's house. They're waiting for us. Come on."

"Warren? Which brother is this?"

"The rancher." London laughed at Ace's frustrated expression. "You'll have fun. He and his wife, Charli, have horses, lots of land. You and my brothers can finally settle the score on who has the better B-ball skills."

"If you think playing basketball with your brothers tops what I want to do with you right now, then, baby, you don't know me as well as I thought."

"I'm sure it doesn't. At least I'd hope so." She reached for his hand and pulled him toward the stairs. "It's just that the sooner we get over there, the sooner we can say our goodbyes and come back here."

"Why in the heck didn't you say so?" Ace picked her up and ran down the stairs. "Let's go!"

Ace's silly antics continued once they got in the car. He sped through the streets of Paradise Cove, his Porsche's wheels hugging the turns. Once they reached the straight-away to Paradise Valley and Warren's ranch he "blew out the car's cobwebs," as his stepfather, Hank, would say. At 140 miles per hour, he ate up the five remaining miles to their destination in just over two minutes flat.

They pulled into a party in full swing. Nannies chased kids running across the Drakes' vast front yard. Music drifted from the backyard, along with the smell of roasting corn and grilling meat. In the backyard, they greeted the crew. Even Reginald and Julian were there. Ace followed London over to where a tall man wearing a cowboy hat expertly flipped a slab of ribs.

"Your brother Warren?"

"How'd you guess?"

Warren turned around. "Hey, London."

"Hey, bro."

"And you must be Ace." Warren wiped his hand against the apron he wore before reaching out to Ace. "Heard you play a little ball."

"Every now and then."

"Well, I've got a full court out back. We'll get a chance to see what kind of player you are, what you're made of."

"Hey, man, the way you're handling that slab of meat, you're my kind of player already!"

"Ha!" Warren looked over at a pretty, slender lady wearing jean shorts, a tee and cowboy boots. "Hey, baby. Do me a favor and get Ace a beer."

The woman reached into a tub filled with bottles and cans, pulled out a beer, brought it over and handed it to Ace.

"Thank you."

"You're welcome. Hey, London."

"Hi, Charli." The women hugged. "Charli, this is Ace."

"So nice to finally meet you."

"It's my pleasure. Are you the one London says rides a horse better than most men?"

"I don't know about all that."

"She's being modest," Warren said. "Girl is one of the baddest horse riders this side of the Mississippi."

"Do you ride?" Charli asked.

"Not horses." Ace kept a straight face. London nudged him.

"London, come with me for a sec. I need your help with something."

"Sure." She kissed Ace's cheek. "Be right back."

London and Charli went inside and walked down a short hallway into a large, airy kitchen that rivaled commercial grade.

"I know you don't cook much," Charli began.

"Make that *at all*."

"Ha! That's okay. You can help me with this part. Just a little slicing and dicing for the macaroni and potato salads." London looked dubious. "It's easy. Promise. I'll give you a little knife."

Charli found a knife in the utensil drawer then pulled a bowl of boiled and peeled eggs, potatoes and pickles from a refrigerator shelf and walked over to a large inlaid cutting board on one of the granite countertops. "Okay, eggs or potatoes, your choice. Dice them any way you want. It's going to be all blended up anyway, so if they're not all uniform it doesn't really matter."

"Okay." She tentatively reached for a boiled egg. "Why didn't you ask Teresa? She would have been a much better choice. I'm all but allergic to kitchens."

"A man likes a woman who can cook, even if it's just a little bit. That fine hunk fawning all over you outside looks worthy of a home-cooked meal."

"I'll hire someone to come over and cook and serve it like I did the job."

Charli started laughing. "You sound serious."

"I am."

London began chopping the eggs. Charli reached for a red onion and did the same. For a few seconds the two focused on the task at hand.

"Actually, there's another reason I wanted you to help me," Charli said. She slid the pile of chopped onions into a bowl.

"What's that? Change your mind about participating in the fashion show?"

"No. That is and will remain a firm no." She placed the knife on the counter and turned to lean against it. "I wanted to share something with you privately."

London stopped chopping at the serious tone. "What?"

"We share some of the same type of pain." Charli placed a comforting hand on London's arm, her voice barely above a whisper. "I, too, was sexually assaulted."

"Did my mom—"

"Please don't blame her, and please don't be mad. I was sharing something with her and it sorta just came out. London, this happens to so many women. When we were in Temecula for Papa Dee's funeral, I learned that another sis-in-law went through the same thing. And then Dexter's wife, the one who established a free clinic in San Diego, shared all of these stories about how prevalent this crime is, and how underreported. Mostly because the victims stay silent. Because of the shame. Did you know that one out of four women are likely to be assaulted during their lifetimes?"

"No, I didn't."

"It's a crazy stat, right?" London nodded. "So anyway, we all decided to be part of the solution and fight back."

"How?"

"We're not sure. A video, PSA, blog… The idea is still very much in the planning stages. It would be great if you'd join us. Your star power would mean everything. I know you're busy and it's a lot to ask, especially since your coming out is so recent, but—"

"I'll do it."

"You will?"

"Absolutely. Since revealing that long-held, shameful secret, my whole life has changed. If I can say something, do something, to get just one young girl to speak up if this crime happens to her, it will give me back some of the power I lost. My predator won't win."

Later that evening, just before Ace and London left the party, she got a phone call.

"Hey, Max."

"Hey there, beautiful. Just called to wish you a happy holiday and to share some news."

"Happy holidays to you, too. What's the news?"

"I just bought a place in Manhattan, the Upper East Side. Over five thousand square feet, skyline views, huge patio. I'm planning a big Fourth of July party to break it in, and I'd love you to join me."

"That sounds amazing, Max. Don't know when I'll see it, though. I haven't gone back to modeling or been traveling a lot lately. It's the most stationary I've been in almost ten years. I'm starting to like it."

"You're still the spokesperson for the Her line, though, right?"

"Yeah, I'm still doing that."

"Then we can hang out during the next fashion week. That's in September, right, when they show the spring lines?"

"You know how busy a time that is, Max. We'll see."

"Ah, come on. No time for a good friend?"

"Sure, why not. We'll have lunch or a drink in Manhattan when I'm there."

London ended the call and literally twirled around the room. She was one of the lucky few to have the best of all worlds: an enviable career, amazing boyfriend and a cordial relationship with the ex who just happened to be a Hollywood A-lister. Maybe she'd make her film debut after all.

No matter the story line, it couldn't rival the fairy tale with Ace that she was living right now. Not a chance.

Chapter 28

What started out as a simple fashion show for charity had grown to a Paradise Cove event not to be missed. Once word got out that London was involved and that the fashions were by OTB Her, ticket sales went through the roof. The venue had changed several times, as had the date. Originally slated for July, it had been moved to December and given a theme: Her for the Holidays.

The summer passed in a blur. London all but moved in with Ace in San Francisco, spending the entire month of August there as they finished the spring line. Now it was September, the month of the four major spring fashion shows. After spending so much time in California, London looked forward to the trip to New York. She and Ace had rented an apartment for the two weeks they'd be there, something she equally looked forward to, since besides fittings, PR appearances and a meeting or two, she'd hardly seen her man.

It was just after noon when the private plane touched down in Manhattan. Fall was very much in the air. A driver whisked them away to Bryant Park and their rented apartment. Ace had to go to work. London had the day off.

"What are you going to do in this big city all by yourself?"

"I thought Jules and I might go shopping."

Jules was the assistant who'd replaced Carly, now living in Los Angeles. Relocated, she said, to pursue an acting career.

"Just remember to be careful, okay?"

"I will. Oh, and I might meet Max for a drink. Please—" she hurried on over Ace's objection "—don't be mad. I put him off all summer and promised to meet him."

"I don't like it, London. More specifically, I don't like him. I don't trust him."

London leaned into Ace's hard chest and slid her arms around his neck. "Trust me," she said huskily, kissing his lips. "You have absolutely nothing to worry about."

"You're not what worries me."

"You still think he's behind that kidnapping, don't you? Why, Ace? The police have never been able to prove who did that or why, and Max is not that kind of guy, I'm telling you."

"You don't think it's strange that after Milan, when you briefly got back with him in Paris, the flowers stopped? The packages stopped. Everything stopped until a month or so after you told him it was over for good. And then came the flowers at OTB. And the diamond necklace delivered to your family's condo."

"Are you forgetting what my dad found out? That my stalker was released early for good behavior and was out and back home in Europe when I was in Paris? That's who I think is behind all of this. And if the detective my dad hired can ever find the guy, I think my theory will be proven correct."

"If you say so." Ace looked at his watch. "Okay, baby. This is the fifth text Frida has sent me. I've got to get over to the space. Don't forget we've got dinner reservations tonight with the editors from *Vogue*."

"I won't forget, babe. See you then."

Ace left. London called Jules. "Hello, Jules. Where are you?"

"In Times Square. Do you need me?"

"Not officially. Thinking about going shopping and want to know if you want to come with."

"I'm here with a couple New Yorker friends of mine. I can come if you want, though."

He said it, but London knew Jules didn't want to leave his friends. She heard it in his voice.

"No problem. Starting tomorrow you'll be joined to my hip, so go ahead and hang out with your friends."

"Are you sure?"

"I'm positive. Have fun."

"Call me if you need me!"

"Will do."

London decided to take a shower and figure out what she wanted to do from there. When she got out, her phone was vibrating. Max.

Instead of returning the text, she called. "Hey, you. What's up?"

"You're what's up, beautiful. Are you here yet?"

"Yep. Just got here a couple hours ago."

"What are you doing right now?"

"Getting dressed. What are you doing?"

"Just finished a meeting in Midtown with a couple producers."

"Where in Midtown? We've rented an apartment near Bryant Park."

"Really? That's perfect. I can come by and swoop you up."

"Too much trouble. Just tell me where you are and I'll catch a cab."

"All right, beautiful. Can't wait to see you."

"Me, too, Max. See you soon."

"Hey, boss, got a minute?" Frida walked over to where Ace huddled with the builders designing the set. "I think we've finally got the invites set. There are just a couple names I need to run by you before I send out their confirmation."

"Let me take a look." Frida handed over her tablet. "Sean Black. Yeah, he's cool. He's a pro baller, starting up his own line. This other name, Brigitte Desrochers?"

"I believe it's pronounced *Bri-geet*, emphasis on the *geet*."

"Don't know her. Did you do a search on her?"

"No, but I can."

"Cool. I'll be over here trying to recreate snow."

Because their rain cylinder had been such a hit, the team's new goal was to fill the runway with powdery snowflakes. Strange juxtaposition for a spring line, but an idea that's indeed out of the box.

Ten minutes later Ace was deep in conversation with the engineer.

"Ace."

He waved Frida off. "Give me a few minutes."

"Okay." She waited fifteen minutes. "Ace, I'm sorry, but I think you should see this."

His immediate scowl confirmed his displeasure. He walked over. "What?"

A party picture filled the screen. He almost snatched the tablet out of her hands. "What's this? Which one is Bridget or Brigeet or whatever her name is?"

"She's right here," Frida said, a shaky finger pointing to a pretty girl at the bar. "But that's not why I'm showing you this picture. Look here, in the corner. That's Carly. All hugged up with and talking to—"

"Maxwell Tata."

Ace was stunned. As he stared at the picture, a mental video began to play. Carly, London's assistant. Who knew all of her information. Traveled to all the cities. He studied the picture again. It had been taken in Paris. Where Max met London. Right after she'd been kidnapped in Milan. Two weeks after fashion week wrapped, Carly had given her resignation. Moved to LA.

Every bad feeling he'd ever had about Max pitted at the bottom of his stomach. *I might meet Max for a drink. Don't be mad. I put him off all summer. We're friends. Max's not that kind of guy. You have absolutely nothing to worry about.*

He pulled out his phone. "London, where are you? Give me a call as soon as you get this. It's important. Call me ASAP."

"...I had dogs in the pool, horses in the yard and a cameraman facedown in the sandpit!"

"Oh, my gosh!" London's eyes teared up she was laughing so hard. This is the Max she'd fallen for: funny, the life of the party.

"What did you do?"

"What else could I do? I yelled 'cut'!"

"Bwa-ha-ha!"

They'd met at a bar near 57th Street owned by an Irishman, a friend of Max's. The crowd was loud and drinks flowed freely, though London refused the offer of a third glass of wine.

"Believe me, after that production wrapped I was ready to leave the West Coast."

"I can understand. The only thing crazier than what you've told me is that it's all true. But seriously, why did you move east?"

"I didn't sell my house in Los Angeles, just went bi-coastal for a couple reasons. The producers I met with earlier have some deep-pocketed investors interested in launching reality-TV shows."

"Really? Ace and I... Never mind."

"Oh, no, go ahead. I meant what I said earlier, London. Your happiness is what matters to me most of all."

"Are you dating?"

"That's the second reason I moved here."

"Oh, really?"

"And it may surprise you that she's neither a model nor an aspiring actor. She's in finance. Works on Wall Street."

"You dating a financier?"

"A very sexy financier."

"I'm happy for you, Max! Why isn't she with us? I'd like to meet her."

"She's working. But she'll be home around five. You can come see my place and meet her, too."

"I don't know, Max. We have dinner reservations for seven. An important meeting."

"We have plenty of time. I'll call her. She'll meet us there and we'll give you a ride back to your place. On the way you can tell me what you and Ace are up to, what you started to say about a reality show. I can see that, by the way. Like I said, the guys I met with are looking to finance projects. They've got connections in Dubai. We're not talking millions—we're talking billions."

* * *

Ace paced their rental home. He was at his wit's end. The calls to London were now going straight to voice mail. Just like what happened in Milan. The feeling that started in the pit of his stomach had spread through his whole body. Something was wrong. London was in trouble. He thought of calling law enforcement. But this was New York. Without some type of evidence other than a feeling, they'd be of little help if they agreed to help at all.

He punched the speaker icon on his phone and tapped a number. "Frida, I need your help. Call the car service to pick me up. Then put on a suit or something official looking and be down in the hotel lobby so we can drive through valet parking to get you."

"Ace, you sound worried. What's this about?"

"No time to explain. Just call the car. I'll tell you when we meet."

London stood in front of a stylish building just blocks from Central Park and waited for Max, who was parking the car. He came around the corner in minutes, unlocked the door and then stepped back to allow her inside. Before her was a beautiful foyer with two-story ceilings, a huge chandelier and marble parquet floors.

"I see why you're so excited to show this place off. I like it, Max. Very nice."

They continued into the massive living room, viewed the dining-kitchen combination along with an office, library and sunroom on the first floor.

"It's nice down here," Max said as they neared the stairs. "But the suite upstairs is where the designers really shined."

They started upstairs.

"Where's your girlfriend? I thought you said you called her when I went to the restroom and she'd be here."

"She's on the way, probably got held up by a last-minute phone call or two. But she's excited to meet you. She'll be here. Don't worry."

They went upstairs. The rooms were everything and more than Max had described.

"This makes me want to buy a place in New York. The designer you hired earned her paycheck."

"A million and a half dollars later, she should have."

After they toured the rest of the second floor, Max wanted them to go to the roof.

London looked at her watch. "I really need to get back to Midtown. Traffic is crazy this time of day. It can take me an hour, easy."

"Just five minutes. Let's go upstairs."

London looked at the short flight of stairs that led to a slanted door. A feeling that she couldn't explain came over her. She'd had an enjoyable afternoon with Max and was glad they could be friendly. But it was time to go.

"Next time, okay? I'm going to leave."

She turned and went down two steps before an iron grip halted her progress. She almost lost her balance and slammed into the wall.

"Max? What are you doing? Let go of my arm!"

"I'll let go of your arm," he said calmly, a blank look in his eyes. "But you're not going anywhere."

London's heart jumped into her throat. Belatedly she realized her purse was on the table in the foyer downstairs. Her cell phone was in it. The fun-loving man with whom she'd shared the last two hours was gone. In his place was someone she'd never seen before. A stranger. A madman. There was no overpowering him. Max wasn't that tall, but he worked out regularly. She couldn't beat him up, so she'd have to try to outsmart him.

"Let's go in the bedroom."

"Excuse me?"

"You heard me. Let's go. I've been wanting to try out the bed in there."

London swallowed her fear and forced a carefree laugh. "Is that what this is about? You want to have sex? You know how good we are together. If you wanted some, all you had to do was ask."

She watched Max's eyes as he processed her statement, half wanting him to believe her, half hoping he wouldn't. There was no way she was going to let this man force himself on her.

One step at a time, London. Keep him calm.

She walked past him up the stairs. "Come on. Which bedroom?"

Max continued to eye her warily. "Let's go downstairs first. I want a drink."

Thank You, God. "Oh, I know. Some champagne for a tongue bath, or maybe some belly shots? Okay, player. Let's go!"

She wanted to full-out sprint in five-inch stilettos but forced herself to take each step slowly, swaying her hips on each stair. They reached the bottom. Max grabbed her, pushed her against the wall and kissed her. Her natural instinct was to resist, but she relaxed her body, slid her arms around his neck and…jabbed her knee into his private parts as hard as she could.

"Aw!"

London grabbed her purse, headed for the door and pulled. Locked. She turned every knob. The door still wouldn't budge.

Max lay sprawled half on the bottom step, half on the

floor. Still in pain he managed to eke out, "This what you're looking for?"

Yes, London thought as she looked at the key dangling from a chain around his neck. It was exactly what she needed.

"There's no way out of here, London. Once I get my strength back, you're going to wish you hadn't kneed me."

"Max, this isn't going to end well. Let me go."

"Unlike what happened in Milan, it's going to end exactly as I want."

Her eyes widened then narrowed. "It was you."

"I had the perfect date planned, better than any romance. But then I got word that people were looking for you, combing the mall, interrogating the hotel staff. I had to get you back there. Your parents coming to town put a crimp in my plans."

"You kidnapped me."

"That's a rather dramatic way to look at it. You'd taunted me for months, giving the impression you'd get back with me. I let you lead for a while and then decided to take control. As a director, it's what I do best."

"Ace thought it was you. I should have believed him."

"I've got a plan for him, too," Max spat out as he struggled to his knees. "But tonight belongs to us."

London took off through the house, looking for a way out. A door, a window—either would do. All she found was a set of double doors and a back door. Both were locked. She swallowed her panic, forced herself to think.

My phone. I've got to get to it before Max gets up.

There was only one problem with this plan. Max had recovered and found her. His hand was now around her neck.

"Max. Stop."

He jerked her arm behind her and started walking

toward the stairs. When they got halfway up, the doorbell rang.

His girlfriend!

"Max, unlock the door for your girlfriend. You don't
want her to see us like this."

"There's no girlfriend. Whoever that is will go away.
Now come on!"

London knew that whoever was at that door was her
lifeline. She wasn't going up the stairway. One way or another, either walking, crawling or falling, they were going
back down.

The doorbell rang again, followed by insistent knock-
ing.

Max growled. "Let me get rid of whoever this is. Try
anything, and you'll regret it."

He looked out of the door pane to see a pretty woman
in a uniform at his door.

"Yeah, who are you!"

"Special delivery," the pretty woman replied.

"From who?"

"A, um, Ms. Tanner, sir. It requires a signature."

London watched Max relax. Carly Tanner, her assistant?
Later she would learn that Carly was the woman who'd
helped him know London's every move. She'd helped him
in Milan. After her stint with OTB ended, he'd hired her
as an assistant of sorts. Someone to help with matters that
had to stay private. Matters to which Maxwell Tata could
not be linked. Like renting a house on New York's Upper
East Side. London would learn all of this later. All she
knew right now was relief as she watched Max crack open
the door.

An unlocked door was all Ace needed. He reached past
Frida, pushed open the door and did what he'd longed
to…introduce his fist to Maxwell's face.

Chapter 29

By the time December and the Her for the Holidays show rolled around, New York City and Maxwell Tata's abduction were a painful but distant memory. London owed her life to Ace. Everything he'd suspected was true. While Carly denied any involvement in the gift sending or kidnapping, she couldn't deny that she knew Max.

London now knew what Ace had believed from the beginning—Maxwell Tata was a very dangerous man. Had Ace not outfitted her phone with a special, high-level tracking system shortly after they'd returned from Europe, a fact that in her terror London had completely forgotten, there was no way he would have found her in the city that never slept. London pressed charges. Max pleaded no contest to unlawful imprisonment. He paid a hefty fine but because of a high-powered attorney with major connections, he didn't spend one night in jail. The best thing that came out of the horrible incident was the

$5 million punitive damage judgment that funded the assault-awareness campaign that she, Charli and a couple cousins who'd also been abused oversaw. She was now not only the face of OTB Her, but the representative of millions of sexually assaulted victims who remained silent. She was their face and their voice.

"Hey, baby."

Ace came up and wrapped his arms around her. They were just behind a sheer curtain in a tent that had been constructed around Drake Lake, which had been transformed into a winter wonderland. An industrious engineering firm had used thick slabs of Plexiglas, steel beams and concrete blocks to bring to life the frozen lake that Ace had imagined when planning the show. In keeping with the signature moves for which OTB Her was now famous, this man-made lake was part of the show's finale.

She turned, straightening the lapels of his OTB tux. "Did anyone ever tell you that you could be a model? You're really handsome. It's a career you should consider."

He squeezed her tighter. "No, I kind of like my position behind the scenes. I'm in love with a beautiful woman who happens to be a model herself. I like to help her career. She shines brighter in the spotlight then I ever could."

London looked over her shoulder. Her heart swelled at the scene behind her. Eight of the finest men in not just Paradise Cove but the world walked toward her, all wearing OTB: Julian, Terrell, Warren, Reginald, Niko, Ike Jr., Ike Sr. and Teresa's husband, Atka Sinclair.

"Look, baby, our escorts!"

Ace turned and nodded slowly. "Look at the Drake men representing."

"And a Sinclair," London said.

Atka shook his head. "Naw, I'm an honorary Drake tonight."

Frida walked over. "We need you guys backstage to help line up the models. The show starts in ten."

Ace looked at the group. "All right, fellas. I'll spare you the backstage zoo and line you guys up just outside the door. As a model comes out, you'll offer her your arm and basically follow her lead. She'll walk to the middle of the runway, pose, to the end, pose and come back."

Ike Sr. looked worried. "Ace, I think we should have rehearsed this."

London walked up to her father, their relationship better than ever. "Just walk when they walk, stop when they stop and leave the stage with them. You'll be fine." She kissed his cheek. "I never thought I'd say this, Dad, but... See you on the runway!"

London peeked around a curtain as her mom addressed the crowd. There'd been no plan to stop and listen but hearing the woman who'd named her Clarisse call her by the name she'd chosen stopped her cold.

"Good evening. Most if not all of you know about my daughter London. You've seen her in magazines, on television and online. She was born and for a while raised right here in Paradise Cove. She's our golden child, with an it factor for as far back as I can remember. She was rambunctious, curious, fearless. Not much has changed. During her teen years, Ike and I sent her to a boarding school, to instill discipline, and smooth her rough edges." Ripples of laughter rolled across the audience. "But what does she do? One-up us by becoming an international supermodel." The audience applauded. "That's our golden child. We couldn't be more proud."

Tears stained London's makeup as she rushed to get into position for the first look.

"And with that, ladies and gentlemen, I invite you to sit back and enjoy Her for the Holidays!"

The fashions were bold, innovative, transformative. Jewel-tone sweaters, slacks and dresses. Double-breasted pantsuits, faux-fur skirts underlaid with crinoline, chaps-inspired gaucho pants with thigh-high cowboy boots. Twenty looks, each more amazing than the last. The applause was continuous. Each look was bid on silently. Sales were through the roof.

London shimmied into the showstopping finale, then stood waiting for her cue. When it came, instead of walking down the runway she came toward the audience from the other side of the lake, ice-skating effortlessly on the rink the engineers had configured in a skintight red leather dress with a wide skirt and train. A lone spotlight directed her path. A murmur began as she neared the crowd, developing into an all-out crescendo by the time she reached them. She glided from one side to the other, twirled and spun to show off the dress. The crowd continued to cheer, then began standing. She knew the ending they'd planned was fantastic, but this reaction was almost too much. She spun around, and to her surprise noticed the crowd's attention was not on her but on another lone skater coming her way. A man in an OTB tux, carrying a single rose.

This hadn't been rehearsed.

Ace neared her, and London's heart nearly beat out of her chest. An expert skater, he too delighted the audience with spins and turns. He came directly at her. She instinctually braced herself for being swept up and around. There was a five-minute fireworks display planned before they were to skate back up for a final bow. He reached for her hand. Together they floated on the ice. The crowd went wild.

She chided him while wearing a smile. "You could have warned me."

"I learned a long time ago that warning you doesn't work." He smiled, took her hand and glided toward where Jennifer stood, cordless microphone in hand, to close the show.

"Ace! What are you doing?"

"You'll know in a minute."

He reached the lake's edge, where the Plexiglas covering jutted onto the grass, hidden beneath fake snow.

Jennifer, obviously confused, held up a finger to the crowd and hurried over.

"Wasn't that the finale?" she whispered. "It was fantastic."

"Almost," Ace replied. He nodded toward the microphone she held. "May I?"

"Of course! Not having you speak was a complete oversight."

She turned to the crowd. "It gives me immense pleasure to formally introduce the wonderful designer of this trendsetting line. Ladies and gentlemen, please give a grand Paradise Cove welcome to Ace Montgomery."

As one, the crowd broke out in wild applause. The clapping slowly subsided. Jennifer gave Ace the mic.

"You guys are amazing," he began. "Mrs. Drake, thank you for allowing me the honor of dressing the beautiful women of Paradise Cove while supporting a worthy cause. And for this generous, enthusiastic crowd. Thank you."

He waited as once again the audience showed their immense appreciation.

"The launch of this line, OTB Her, was successful because of the innovative and inspired designs of a creative and talented fashion team. But they are only part of the reason. The other reason women all over the world are clamoring for these garments is the woman standing beside me and the carefree, confident spirit she exudes every time she walks the runway. One of your own, Paradise Cove... London Drake!"

His public admission of her part in OTB Her's success was totally unexpected and warmed London's heart. That and the applause, yells and whistles from the crowd of mostly Paradise Cove residents acknowledging one of their own. Because of her time away from the town, she'd never really felt a connection. Tonight, for the first time, Paradise Cove truly felt like home.

Ace extended the microphone toward her.

"Thank you, everybody, especially my mom, dad and all of my brothers and sisters. Having all of you take a walk in my world is something I will never forget. This night has been amazing."

"One last thing," Ace began as the applause died down. "Something else was launched during the unveiling of OTB Her." He stopped, looking at London.

"A love affair."

London's eyes widened. Since the kidnapping, they'd made no effort to hide the fact that they were dating. But they hadn't broadcast it, either. She stood enraptured by his gaze, touched by the love she saw there. She barely heard the murmuring audience, was only vaguely aware that her sister, Teresa, snapped a series of pictures and through her popular blog would be the first to report this breaking news.

"We met years ago," Ace finally continued. "It was a brief encounter after which we went our separate ways. I let her get away that time. When fate brought us together again, I remembered one of the many lessons my mom, a schoolteacher, taught me—don't make the same mistake twice."

He turned to London. "You've walked from the runway right into my heart. I want to keep you here forever." Whistles and applause erupted as Ace pulled out a box and knelt on one knee. He popped open the box and revealed a five-carat yellow diamond ring.

"Clarisse Alana London Drake…will you marry me?"

London looked into the face of the love of her life and answered the same as when he'd asked her to be the face of OTB Her. "I'll think about it."

Jaws dropped. The crowd buzzed. A mixture of surprise and disappointment peeked through the mask Ace now wore.

"Okay, thought about it," she continued after only seconds had passed. "Get up, Ace Montgomery. My answer is yes!"

The smile on his face could have lit up the world. He stood, took London in his arms and swirled them around and around. One again the audience clapped and cheered. Cameras flashes went off in every direction. Ace handed a stunned yet pleased Jennifer the microphone and reached for London's hand. They waved a final goodbye and skated behind the stage to the ramp that led to the makeshift dressing room.

Their job was done. London felt complete. She'd contributed to the Drakes' good name and brand. Her for the Holidays had been a rousing success. Because she'd just said yes to her man, Ace Montgomery was going to be hers forever, along with a lifetime of lavish loving. The show had been perfect, but what an encore!

* * * * *

SPECIAL EXCERPT FROM

She's got sky-high ambitions to match the glamorous penthouses she shows, but real estate agent Angela Trainor keeps both feet firmly on the ground. Her attraction to her sexy boss, Daniel Cobb, needs to remain at bay or it could derail her promising career. But when Daniel takes Angela under his wing, their mutual admiration could become a sizzling physical connection...

Read on for a sneak peek at
MIAMI AFTER HOURS,
the first exciting installment of
Harlequin Kimani Romance's continuity
MILLIONAIRE MOGULS OF MIAMI!

"Now you just have to seal the deal and get to closing." He knew that just because an offer had been made didn't mean the sale was a foregone conclusion. Deals could fall apart at any time. Not that it ever happened to him. Daniel took every precaution to ensure that it didn't.

"Of course."

"Speaking of deals, I've recently signed a new client, a developer that has tasked me with selling out the eighty condos in his building in downtown Miami."

Angela's eyes grew large. "Sounds amazing."

"It is, but it's a challenge. The lower-end condos go for a thousand a square foot, and the penthouse is fifteen hundred a square foot."

"Well, if anyone can do it, you can."

Daniel appreciated her ego boost. "Thank you, but praise is not the reason I'm mentioning it."

"No?" She quirked a brow and he couldn't resist returning it with a grin.

"I want you to work on the project with me."

"You do?" Astonishment was evident in her voice.

"Why do you think I plucked you away from that other firm? It was to give you the opportunity to grow and to learn under my tutelage."

"I'm ready for whatever you want to offer me." She blushed as soon as she said the words, no doubt because he could certainly take it to mean something other than work. Something like what he could offer her in the bedroom.

Where had that thought come from?

It was his cardinal rule to never date any woman in the workplace. Angela would be no different. He didn't mix business with pleasure.

He banished the thought and finally replied, "I'm sure you are." Then he walked over to his desk, procured a folder and handed it to her. "Read this. It'll fill you in on the development. Let's plan on putting our heads together on a marketing strategy tomorrow after you've had time to digest it."

Angela nodded and walked toward the door. "And, Daniel?"

"Yes?"

"Thank you for the opportunity."

Don't miss MIAMI AFTER HOURS
by Yahrah St. John, available June 2017
wherever Harlequin® Kimani Romance™
books and ebooks are sold.

Copyright © 2017 by Harlequin Books S.A.

KPEXP0517

Get 2 Free Books,
Plus 2 Free Gifts—
just for trying the
Reader Service!

YES! Please send me 2 FREE Harlequin® Kimani™ Romance novels and my 2 FREE gifts (gifts are worth about $10 retail). After receiving them, if I don't wish to receive any more books, I can return the shipping statement marked "cancel." If I don't cancel, I will receive 4 brand-new novels every month and be billed just $5.69 per book in the U.S. or $6.24 per book in Canada. That's a savings of at least 12% off the cover price. It's quite a bargain! Shipping and handling is just 50¢ per book in the U.S. and 75¢ per book in Canada.* I understand that accepting the 2 free books and gifts places me under no obligation to buy anything. I can always return a shipment and cancel at any time. Even if I never buy another book, the 2 free books and gifts are mine to keep forever.

168/368 XDN GLQK

Name	(PLEASE PRINT)	
Address		Apt. #
City	State/Prov.	Zip/Postal Code

Signature (if under 18, a parent or guardian must sign)

Mail to the **Reader Service:**
IN U.S.A.: P.O. Box 1867, Buffalo, NY 14240-1867
IN CANADA: P.O. Box 611, Fort Erie, Ontario L2A 9Z9

Want to try two free books from another line?
Call 1-800-873-8635 or visit www.ReaderService.com.

*Terms and prices subject to change without notice. Prices do not include applicable taxes. Sales tax applicable in NY. Canadian residents will be charged applicable taxes. Offer not valid in Quebec. This offer is limited to one order per household. Books received may not be as shown. Not valid for current subscribers to Harlequin®Kimani™ Romance books. All orders subject to credit approval. Credit or debit balances in a customer's account(s) may be offset by any other outstanding balance owed by or to the customer. Please allow 4 to 6 weeks for delivery. Offer available while quantities last.

Your Privacy—The Reader Service is committed to protecting your privacy. Our Privacy Policy is available online at www.ReaderService.com or upon request from the Reader Service.

We make a portion of our mailing list available to reputable third parties that offer products we believe may interest you. If you prefer that we not exchange your name with third parties, or if you wish to clarify or modify your communication preferences, please visit us at www.ReaderService.com/consumerschoice or write to us at Reader Service Preference Service, P.O. Box 9062, Buffalo, NY 14240-9062. Include your complete name and address.

KROM17R

A royal seduction

A.C. ARTHUR

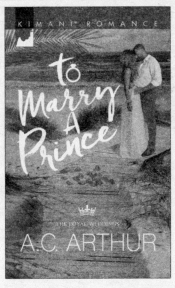

Never one to lose control, crown prince Kristian DeSaunters is stunned by his attraction to free-spirited American stylist Landry Norris. Soon they're sharing a sultry attraction, until someone sets out to destroy the DeSaunters's reign. Will they be able to stop a hidden enemy and save their future together?

THE ROYAL WEDDINGS

Available May 2017!

"Hot and heavy love scenes, an inspiring heroine and a well-balanced story line full of drama, secrets and passion will keep readers on their toes from start to finish."
— *RT Book Reviews* on *SURRENDER TO A DONOVAN*

H HARLEQUIN®
www.Harlequin.com

KPACA521

A hero's touch

SHERYL LISTER

KIMANI™ ROMANCE

Giving My all to You

THE GRAYS OF LOS ANGELES

SHERYL LISTER

Brandon Gray's focus is on the long-coveted role of CEO—until he helps a mysterious beauty. Ever since a car accident, Faith Alexander's rescuer has been by her side. With chemistry this irresistible, how can she reveal that her inheritance stands in the way of his dreams?

THE GRAYS *of* LOS ANGELES

Available May 2017!

"This tale hits on every emotional level and will leave readers feeling inspired, romantic and thoroughly satisfied."
—*RT Book Reviews* on *It's Only You*

HARLEQUIN®
www.Harlequin.com

KPSL522